WAYNE STINNETT

RECKLESS CHARITY

A CHARITY STYLES NOVEL

Caribbean Thriller Series
Volume 3

DOWN ISLAND PRESS

2017

Published by DOWN ISLAND PRESS, 2017
Travelers Rest, SC
Copyright © 2017 by Wayne Stinnett

Library of Congress cataloging-in-publication Data
Stinnett, Wayne
Reckless Charity/Wayne Stinnett
p. cm. - (A Charity Styles novel)
ISBN-10: 0-9981285-4-6 (Down Island Press)
ISBN-13: 978-0-9981285-4-2

Cover Photo by Niknikon
Graphics by Wicked Good Book Covers
Edited by Tammi at Larks & Katydids
Final Proofreading by Donna Rich
Interior Design by Colleen Sheehan, WDR Book Designs

This is a work of fiction. Names, characters, and incidents are either the product of the author's imagination or are used fictitiously. Any resemblance to actual persons, living or dead, businesses, companies, events, or locales is entirely coincidental.

Most of the locations herein are also fictional, or are used fictitiously. However, I took great pains to depict the location and description of the many well-known islands, locales, beaches, reefs, bars, and restaurants in the Keys, to the best of my ability.

FOREWORD

Many thanks, first and always, to my wife, Greta. Your unerring support and dedication has been the backbone of my success in whatever I try.

My beta reading team always provides great feedback and advice. These folks don't look for typos and grammatical errors, that's the editor's job. Instead, they look for plot holes and dead ends. Writing takes a long time and often the writer will include something that either doesn't go anywhere or doesn't match up with previous works in the series. My beta readers go over the manuscript more than once, looking for just these mistakes. What takes months to write, only takes hours to read and they find all the little problems, even suggesting subtle changes for a better read. Such was the case when I wrote the scene with the bomb. John Trainor saw that what I'd written was similar to a quote from Shakespeare, so I rewrote the scene using the quote, which gives Victor more depth. Much gratitude is owed to Mike Ramsey, Katy McKnight, Dr. John Trainor, Marcus Lowe, Dana Vihlen, Karl Schulte, Debbie Kocol, Dave Parsons, Ron Ramey, Gary Cox, and Charles Hofbauer.

Trying to capture a feeling in words is not easy. Sailing is an experience that encompasses many emotions. In these books, I try to let Charity describe her feelings and love of the sea just enough to make her real in the eyes of those of you who live the cruising lifestyle, but not so much that it detracts from the story. I hope that I found the balance.

DEDICATION

To my brother, Mike. Only sixteen months apart in age, we were competitors in everything. Backyard football, chess, swimming; anything that two boys could do, we did it together, constantly driving the other to do better. Later, we stood back-to-back in quite a few scrapes. His birthday was just a few weeks ago and he's now joined me in the "late-fifties" club. Take a look around, bro. We're miles ahead of the pack.

"You don't have to be someone special to achieve something amazing. You've just got to have a dream, believe in it and work hard."
- **Jessica Watson** - *Youngest person to sail around the world, alone and unassisted.*

If you'd like to receive my twice a month newsletter for specials, book recommendations, and updates on coming books, please sign up on my website:

WWW.WAYNESTINNETT.COM

THE CHARITY STYLES
CARIBBEAN THRILLER SERIES

Merciless Charity
Ruthless Charity
Reckless Charity

THE JESSE MCDERMITT
CARIBBEAN ADVENTURE SERIES

Fallen Out
Fallen Palm
Fallen Hunter
Fallen Pride
Fallen Mangrove
Fallen King
Fallen Honor
Fallen Tide
Fallen Hero
Rising Storm (Summer, 2017)

The Gaspar's Revenge Ship's Store is now open. There you can purchase all kinds of swag related to my books.
WWW.GASPARS-REVENGE.COM

MAPS

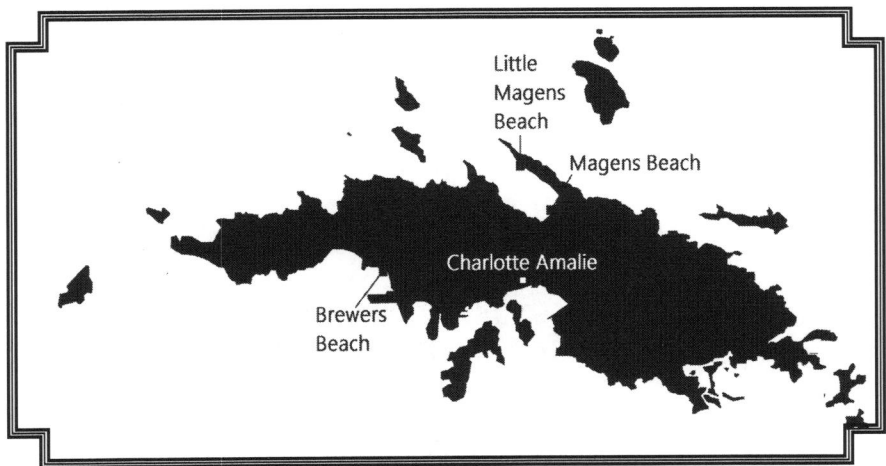

St. Thomas Island, USVI

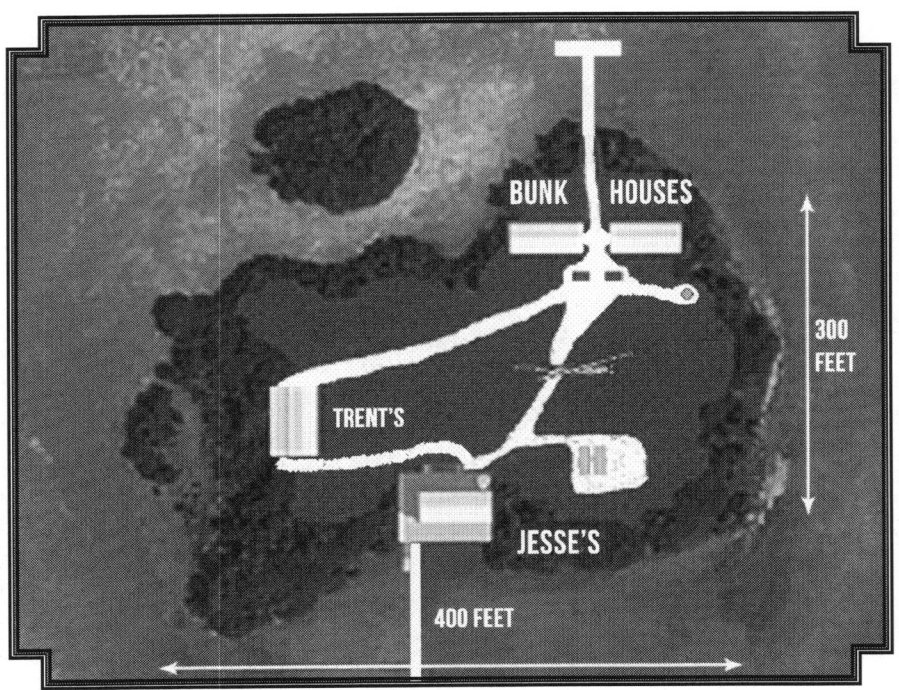

Jesse's Island

RECKLESS
CHARITY

CHAPTER ONE:

Tiny waves lapped gently at the coarse, yellow-white sand. They seemed more like the tiny ripples you'd see in a small pond, after tossing a pebble. Just a few yards from the beach, the water of the bay turned a deep blue as the bottom quickly dropped away. Further up the shore, toward the foot of the long, rocky point that protected the bay, several good-sized fishing boats were beached, unloading their catch.

Around three sides of the bay, craggy volcanic rock rose right out of the water in most places. Aside from this quarter-mile-long shore, there were only a handful of other sand beaches in the bay, all very small. Magens Bay, the largest bay on the island of Saint Thomas, and Magens Beach, arguably one of its largest beaches, were rarely crowded—even in the height of tourist season, which hadn't yet begun.

This was to a certain degree due to its exposure to the sometimes treacherous North Atlantic. Magens Bay was a cruising destination, popular for its panoramic views and quiet tranquility. Most of the tourists stayed on the south side of the island, to be close to the nightlife of Charlotte Amalie. Though they were only a few miles apart, mountains separated Magens Bay from the more popular anchorages to the south.

Normally, the bay would have had at least two dozen cruisers, mostly sailboats, anchored just off the north end of the beach, where the fishermen were unloading. But three days ago a late-season hurricane had passed within two hundred miles of the Virgin Islands, so the bay was empty. The fishermen had only returned to work the day before.

Moving Wind Dancer *was a waste of time*, Charity thought as she gazed out over the water. The storm had never come any closer than two hundred miles, and its forward speed had been enough that it didn't kick up large waves on Saint Thomas. Still, moving *Wind Dancer* had been the prudent thing to do. Living on a boat, you didn't mess around with hurricanes.

"One comes this way, you go that way," a salty old sailor had told her, just before weighing anchor and heading south out of the path of Hurricane Ike.

So she'd moved the *Dancer* to a slip at Yacht Haven Grande, a large marina on the more protected south side of the island.

Charity had come to Saint Thomas to unwind, work on her tan, and be alone—and for the last two days, she'd been forced to ride her bike for miles to find a secluded beach.

Starting early this morning, she'd ridden the three miles from the marina to check on the anchorage in Magens Bay. Not a long ride on her folding bike, but the route across the island wound its way through the higher mountains. The pass on Hull Bay Road, roughly the halfway point of the ride, was nearly a thousand feet above sea level.

Charity spread a towel on the deserted beach and dropped her pack next to it. She took a long pull from a water bottle as she slowly looked around. Aside from the fishermen several hundred yards away, the beach and the bay were completely devoid of people. She pulled off her tee-shirt and shorts, then stretched out on the towel wearing the yellow bikini she'd bought in Aruba several months before. The towel was already warm from the sand, and the sun felt hot on her skin. Occasionally, a puff of a breeze out of the north would rustle the coconut palms and cause her exposed flesh to prickle.

"I'll move back here tomorrow," she said aloud and closed her eyes.

The late summer air hung heavily, and the warm sun lulled Charity to a more relaxed state than she'd been in many weeks. Her mind wandered back over the past eighteen months, since she'd left the States headed for an encounter with a terrorist cell on a volcano on the Mexican mainland. She'd been sent there to kill the leader, but she'd killed the whole cell in a bloodthirsty rage.

Since then, there had been several more missions, and she'd crossed the Caribbean in all directions. She preferred to sail *Dancer* to each one, but occasionally she flew a helicopter that was currently stored at a private airfield in Puerto Rico.

She'd been reprimanded after that first mission, but more work had soon come her way. She'd been sent after a land baron in Venezuela, a cartel kingpin in Colombia, and a gang leader in Jamaica; she'd even kidnapped a couple right out from under Fidel and Raul's noses in Cuba.

The Cuba mission had come very close to getting her killed, so she'd requested a month of rest and relaxation.

Her missions now were a lot different than the ones she'd participated in, while working under DHS. There, she'd worked with a whole team of highly skilled operators, each sharing his or her expertise with the other members of the Caribbean Counter-terrorism Command.

Now she worked alone, completely unfettered by responsibilities for others or ridiculous rules of engagement that gave the enemy a huge advantage. In the near future, she'd be given another target; soon after, that person would die. She had no illusions about what she was doing, nor about her own abilities.

Well-trained in hand-to-hand fighting, Charity had taught krav maga to her former teammates. She'd learned the Israeli combat fighting technique while convalescing from injuries she received in Afghanistan, then continued her training after returning home and taking a job as a Miami-Dade patrol officer.

Through her DHS counterparts, she'd mastered other skills and weapons, as well.

And she had wiles that could disarm her target, and looks that could distract any man—as she'd done in Colombia. There, she'd had to get in close and kill the man with a fast-acting poison. The two days she'd spent inside his compound—and in his bed—would have nauseated her, but for the knowledge that he would die as soon as he let his guard down.

Later, in Cuba, Charity had sensed that she was losing her edge. She wasn't as focused as she normally was, and that lack of focus had nearly cost her life. Inwardly, she readily admitted to herself that only the killing of the terrorists had been satisfying. But she would never tell anyone else that.

Since then, her missions had been more against enemies of the CIA than against enemies of the state. She was unsure how much longer she could continue, or even if she should. Her reassignment was supposed to be more about fighting the country's enemies on their terms, which were no terms at all. No rules—kill or be killed, any way she could get it done.

Her nightmares had all but ceased after Mexico; the demons that had once prowled her mind while she slept were for the most part dormant. She'd always been able to compartmentalize her conscious mind, to put the bad things that had happened to her under a mental lock and key. She'd openly confided in one of her former teammates, a man with whom she'd spent several weeks tracking down a traitorous killer. She'd told him about her nightmares and everything that had happened to her when she'd been captured in Afghanistan.

She'd never told anyone else everything that had happened—not even her shrinks, though she did have to give them *something*. She couldn't very well tell them that her Taliban captors had provided sweet tea and fresh linens on her bed, but she also couldn't tell them that for the first twenty-four hours her "bed" had been the table she was tied face down on while she was repeatedly raped and sodomized.

She'd told all these things to Jesse McDermitt, during their weeks alone on his boat. She'd sensed that he was plagued by his own demons, and he was the kind of man that could draw things out. He'd told her not to fight against the demons, but to embrace them and bend them to her own will. He'd shown her how she was stronger than them—and he'd been right.

She'd soon learned to control things much better, tempering her desire to slaughter the enemy with a methodical approach and selective targeting. Jesse had once trained Marine snipers, and was a good teacher and role model of self-discipline—and when it came to the rifle, she'd learned later, there was no equal. He'd taught the team not just the art of shooting accurately at long distances, but also how to use cover and concealment in many forms.

Charity missed the friends she'd made. She wondered all the time what they were doing—if they remembered her, or talked about her.

The sound of a splash brought her back to the moment. She propped herself up on her elbows and looked out over the serene bay. There was a sailboat anchored about fifty yards off the north end of the beach, with a man on the bow securing the anchor chain.

She must have dozed. The entrance to the bay was a mile and a half away, and the bay had been empty when she'd lied down in the sun. The boat was big—bigger than *Wind Dancer* by about ten feet in length, with a cutter-ketch rig and the beamy look and high freeboard of a passage-making blue-water cruiser. She recognized the lines of the small ship, a Formosa.

She also recognized the man on the bow.

Quickly, she gathered her towel, clothes, and backpack, and walked toward the trees where she'd left her bike. She didn't move fast enough to draw attention—at least, she hoped not. She walked nonchalantly toward the trees and didn't look back until she was out of sight of the boat.

Behind a flowering bush, Charity stopped and moved a branch slightly for a better view. Victor Pitt was looking in her direction through a pair of binoculars, scanning the tree line. She was certain he couldn't see her through the brush, with its bright yellow flowers. But had he recognized her as she walked away with her back to him?

Her hair was now close to its natural blond, so she doubted the fugitive CIA agent recognized her. She'd been a brunette—and he'd been Rene Cook—when she'd met him on the island of Trinidad, over a year ago.

Slowly, Victor lowered the field glasses and went back to the aft cockpit, disappearing below deck. Charity quickly pulled her shorts and tee-shirt on over her bathing suit, shouldered her pack, and grabbed her bicycle, hurrying toward the road that would take her back to Charlotte Amalie and *Wind Dancer*.

Pumping hard up the trail leading to the high pass, she released her body to the task of riding the steep ascent and thought about the man she'd just seen. They'd shared a bed, more than once—even after they'd each known who the other really was. He'd helped her on her mission into the jungles of Venezuela, had even taken a bullet in doing so. Then he'd disappeared like a puff of smoke.

She grinned slightly, remembering that he'd told her that had been his code name before deserting the Agency: Smoke.

What's he doing here? Magens Bay was just the kind of place Victor would choose, if he were still on the run. Secluded and isolated, visited by cruisers who mostly wanted to be left alone. *Could that be all there is?*

Charity Styles wasn't the kind of woman who slunk away from an altercation, but she'd also learned patience. If an altercation was unavoidable, a smart operator would make it on their own ground and at a time of their own choosing.

She would move *Wind Dancer* back to Magens Bay and confront Victor Pitt, but not today—and not at a time when he could see her coming. Today, she'd go back to the marina and make ready to sail. It was only fifteen or twenty miles around the western tip of the island; it wouldn't take long, even if she had to run the diesel engine the whole way. There was no chance that Victor might stumble upon her at the marina. She'd go to sleep early and leave after midnight, so it would still be dark when she dropped anchor in Magens Bay.

As she reached the pass, the ground leveled off for a few yards. Charity stopped for a moment to look down at the bay. The area where Victor was anchored was obscured by trees, but the high pass had a commanding view of the bay's entrance and Hans Lollik Island just to the north.

She chugged half a bottle of water, then leaned over and poured the rest over her head and neck, letting the water cascade down over her face. Though it was warm from hours in the backpack, it cooled her. She flipped her hair back to sling off most of the water, then got back on the little bike and coasted down the hill toward Long Bay and the marina.

The afternoon sun had heated *Dancer's* interior, so Charity opened all the hatches and went back up on deck to store the bike and let the cabin cool down. In the cockpit, she powered up the chart plotter and plotted a course around the western tip of Saint Thomas.

Wind Dancer had a five-and-a-half-foot draft, and there were shoal waters to avoid. A forty-five-foot cutter-rigged sloop, designed by John Alden himself, she'd been built in a small shipyard in Maine in 1932, and refitted nearly two years ago. With her modern technology and amenities, *Wind Dancer* was easily single-handed. She had electronics that controlled virtually everything onboard, and she could sail herself across the Pacific. With her thirty-nine-foot waterline, she was easily capable of a sustained speed over eight knots—not fast by powerboat standards, but she had no engine failure worries. The bulk of her eighty-gallon fuel tank was used to power the auxiliary generator, to keep the batteries charged on cloudy, windless days, when the solar panels and wind generator were useless.

With her course plotted, Charity went below to eat a light lunch. She'd bought provisions and refueled when she brought *Dancer* around from Magens Bay, so there was little else to do but go to sleep early.

In the forward berth, Charity stripped down and stepped into the tiny head, turning the water on full hot. Minutes later, her skin raw from the heat and scrubbing, she stretched out nude on the bunk and was soon asleep.

The alarm woke Charity from a sound slumber. It was the middle of the night. As always, she was instantly awake and fully alert. She dressed quickly in dark jeans and a work shirt. Out of habit, she made her bunk, then went to the galley to put the coffee on. While it brewed, she powered up her laptop and connected to the secure satellite. She had no messages, but checking often had also gotten to be a habit. There really was no time off in her line of work. She could be called on to move at a moment's notice, and was always prepared.

Mug and thermos in hand, she started the engine and went up to the cockpit while it warmed up. The little Yanmar diesel made a gentle burbling sound, the only thing to be heard in the marina at this hour. Looking around, she saw nobody on the docks, and none of the other boats' lights were on.

Placing her mug and thermos on the aft bench seat, Charity quickly untied the dock lines. In minutes, she was slowly chugging out of the marina, turning the bow toward the southwest to go around Hassel Island and the much larger Water Island.

With the flip of a couple of switches in the small wheel console, the mainsail and jib silently deployed, catching the easterly breeze off the port quarter. Charity shut off the engine, relishing the silent movement of her craft. It was always a rush to her senses when her boat transferred power from the engine to sail.

The sails snatched at the light wind, heeling the boat over a few degrees. Sunrise was still five hours away, but with just the main and jib she was sailing at a good six knots. There was no need to set the staysail; at this speed she'd enter Magens Bay in about three hours.

At the helm, she sipped her coffee and looked up at the night sky as the lights of the harbor town slipped away to the stern. Due south, just beyond the star-lit horizon, lay Saint Croix. The smart thing to do would be to sail there—or anywhere else, really.

Charity didn't think Victor was a threat to her, though. And he was the first person she'd seen in months that she knew.

Charity sailed around the tip of Water Island and jibed west, then northwest. She engaged the autopilot, and the computer adjusted the sails slightly, following the line on the chart plotter and making for the passage between Kalkun Cay and Salt Cay.

Nearly three hours later, Charity disengaged the autopilot as the computer turned *Dancer* into Magens Bay once more. Studying the bay, Charity stealthily guided *Wind Dancer* into the protected waters. *Dancer*'s hull was a deep blue and her sails chocolate brown, nearly invisible against the dark horizon as the boat silently moved across the water.

She steered toward the spot where the rocky spit joined the mainland of the island at the north end of Magens Beach. Victor's big Formosa was still there and she watched it carefully. There were no lights on and she saw no movement on deck.

Finally, only a few hundred yards from his boat, Charity toggled a switch and the sails rolled silently back into their furlers. Drifting slowly forward, she waited until *Dancer* had nearly stopped before she released the brake on the windlass. The heavy anchor splashed into the water.

The light wind dropped down from the headland and slowly pushed *Dancer* back and away from the Formosa. Charity checked the depth and let the drift pull more of the chain from the closet until she had the right scope out. She engaged the windlass brake and felt the backward momentum stop as the anchor bit into the sandy bottom and pulled the bow around into the wind.

Quickly, Charity went forward and secured the windlass. When that was done, she went below, doused all but the anchor light on the masthead, and sat down at the navigation station. She moved the cursor on the laptop to the camera icon and activated the newly installed remote camera, mounted on the very top of the masthead. The camera could be rotated in a complete circle, giving her a three-hundred-sixty-degree view.

Turning the camera, she studied Victor's boat again, moving the camera slightly as the *Dancer* swung back and forth in the light breeze. There still weren't any lights on. She switched to thermal imaging, but the big boat's thick hull couldn't be penetrated enough to show people inside. It did show the aft section slightly warmer than the rest of the boat. The three big, square portholes on the stern practically glowed, indicating it probably had an aft stateroom and that was likely where Victor was.

She zoomed the camera out, so that the whole boat and then some was in the frame and switched the optics back to night vision, knowing that the man was an early riser. Using only the subdued red light over the galley, she prepared breakfast and started another pot of coffee to drink while she waited.

The wait was less than an hour. As she cleaned the dishes and put them away, a bright light appeared on the laptop screen. She sat down and switched the camera to normal optics. Light poured from the portholes, illuminating long ovals of water around Victor's boat. The eastern sky was starting to brighten, and provided more than enough light for the camera's sensitive optics.

"Okay, Vic," Charity muttered. "Let's see how long it takes before you get curious."

Opening a drawer under the desk, she reached her hand all the way in and pressed a small recess in the corner. The back of the drawer flopped down and she extracted her Sig Sauer P229 and a loaded magazine. Knowing how well sound transferred to water through the wood hull, she quietly inserted the magazine, and without taking her eyes off the screen, slowly racked a round into the chamber, easing the slide back into place. Decocking it, she placed the gun beside the laptop, then reached back into the drawer, removed a clip-on holster, and closed both the hidden panel and the drawer.

Charity holstered the Sig and clipped the holster to her belt. She doubted that Victor being there was anything more than coincidence—and she didn't feel he was a threat in any way—but he was a former CIA operative and a dangerous man. Who knew how he might have changed since they first met?

Ten minutes later, Victor came out of the hatch into his cockpit and looked right at the *Dancer* laying at anchor less than fifty yards away. After a moment, he pulled a pair of binoculars from under a bench and studied Charity's boat from stem to stern.

Victor had never been aboard *Wind Dancer*, Charity had never mentioned her boat's name or what it looked like, and he'd never seen her on it. But they'd both been docked at the same marina in the Caymans when they first met, so he might very well remember having seen the *Dancer* before.

Victor lowered the binoculars and scratched at the stubble of beard on his chin as he gazed at the *Dancer*.

Charity zoomed the camera in on his face. Aside from the week-old beard, he hadn't changed much. She still found him ruggedly handsome.

He seemed to come to a decision and quickly went below. A moment later, he emerged and went to the stern, where his tender was tied. Charity felt a rush of excitement as he glanced at her boat again before pulling the dinghy up to the port side and stepping down into it.

Though it had an engine, Victor set the oars in the dinghy's oarlocks and began rowing. This troubled Charity. Was he trying to approach quietly? She followed him with the camera, as he circled wide around *Wind Dancer's* stern. He was wearing shorts and a tee-shirt, typical of the boating crowd. It didn't appear that he was armed.

Charity reached over to the electrical panel and flipped on the lights in the forward vee-berth. Victor stopped rowing for a moment and finally turned toward Charity's boat. He swept the oars twice, then stood up and hailed her: "Ahoy, *Wind Dancer!*"

Charity didn't hesitate. Victor's guard was down. She went up the ladder to the cockpit and quickly stepped up onto the port bench, her left hand on the boom and her right resting easily on the Sig.

"Sleeping late these days, Victor?" she asked in a barely audible voice.

He nearly stumbled back, but caught his balance before going overboard. "Who is that?" he asked, also in a hushed voice.

He couldn't see her face. With her boat pointed into the easterly breeze, the gathering early morning light was just over her left shoulder, so what little light the rising sun provided was behind her.

But the outline of the gun on her right hip would be clearly visible.

"You've forgotten Port of Spain already?" she asked.

Bending and trying to get a better look, Victor said, "Charity?"

"Why are you here, Victor?"

"Why am I—what? You think I'm after you now? Why are *you* here?"

"I've been here for days," she replied, recalling his paranoia. "Watched you anchor yesterday, so I thought I'd bring my boat around and say hi. Why are you here?"

The sky was getting lighter by the second. Soon, it would be fully daylight. Twilight lasts only a few minutes on the ocean.

Charity could see Victor's eyes as he looked to his right, toward shore, and then to the left, toward his boat.

"Jeez, you're a paranoid shit," she said. "If I *were* here to kill you, you'd already be dead. You know I don't play games."

Slowly, Victor sat down on the tiny bench. "I used to come here pretty regularly. I have friends here. Been up on Andros for the last year or so, working for an old guy who does fishing charters."

"Someone figured out who you were?"

"Something like that."

"Want some coffee?" Charity asked, turning her back and stepping down off the bench to the port rail.

Victor hesitated, then began rowing toward where Charity stood. He rowed backward, ostensibly so he could watch where he was going. But Charity knew it was also due to an overabundance of caution.

When he was close, he tossed the painter and Charity caught it. *Wind Dancer's* cockpit was small, and Charity stepped back as far as she could as Victor stood, put his palms flat on the side deck, and levered himself up.

He stood and faced her, lifting his tee-shirt and turning. "I don't have a gun."

"I know," she replied casually. "What I don't know is if you're still running—or maybe hooked up with one of the many enemies I've made since we last saw each other."

"Hooked up with—" he began, then a light seemed to go on behind his eyes. "I didn't even know that was you on the beach yesterday. You're a blonde now. No, I'm not hooked up with anyone in that way, and not even considering it. I just want to be left alone."

"Except when you don't," Charity said with a grin, remembering that one wild night in her hotel room. "Coffee's in the salon."

As she started to step down into the cabin, a roaring explosion split the calm, morning air.

Dozens of roosting birds flew up from the trees, all screaming together, as Victor and Charity took cover on the deck. Both instinctively reached for their weapons, but only Charity was armed. She drew her Sig from its holster as they lay flat on the deck, faces only inches apart.

On the beach, back among the trees, a rolling cloud of orange flame and black smoke rose into the sky, igniting the branches of several palm trees, which crackled like mini-firecrackers. She'd stopped at the little Tiki bar a few times. It sat just inside the trees, where the road climbed up to the ridge and ran out to the end of the long spit of land, a gathering place for tourists and a spot for locals to exchange information. The old man who owned it made the best conch fritters she'd ever eaten.

"Come on!" Victor said, scrambling over the side to his dinghy and untying the line. As Charity climbed down, he lowered the engine and pulled on the starting cord. It fired up instantly. In the back of her mind, Charity wondered why he'd rowed over if his engine worked.

"That's Chet's shack," he said, twisting the throttle, and running the little boat quickly toward shore. Along Peterborg Peninsula, lights were coming on in the nearer rental villas. A few people came out on their back decks to see what was going on. From up the road leading away from the beach, angry voices could be heard shouting.

Victor ran his dinghy right up on the beach at full speed, only shutting off the engine as the prop came up out of the water, and grabbed a fire extinguisher from under the little console. Together, he and Charity sprinted toward the fire.

Charity could see that the little Tiki bar was completely destroyed, what was left of it ablaze in an alcohol-fueled inferno. Through the trees, she could see a group of men in the firelight. One was on the ground, and three others were kicking and screaming at him. She veered off toward them as Victor began dousing the fire with the extinguisher.

The three men turned as one when Charity crashed through the brush into the clearing. None appeared to be armed. Not wanting to explain to anyone why she was shooting people, she quickly holstered her gun and walked toward them, her strides long and purposeful.

"Ain't nutting for yuh here, white bitch," one of the men said, as he separated himself from the other two. Then he grinned and looked at his friends. "But maybe dis pretty thing wanna dance wit all three of us."

The other two men spread out a little. They were young black men, long hair twisted into dreadlocks—more popular on Jamaica than in the Virgin Islands. Their accents didn't sound like those of the people here on Saint Thomas. All three were capable looking.

A second man grinned. "Ya mon, let's take dis bitch up to di shack and dance all day. Dat what yuh want, white girl? Three big bulls to dance yuh pretty ass on?"

The man they'd been kicking scurried a few feet away like a crab as Charity closed the distance. The second man to speak was closest and charged at her, arms wide, like he was trying to catch a chicken.

Charity moved instinctively, fluidly stepping in and ducking under the man's outstretched arm without breaking stride. It was a move she'd taught her former teammates, one she'd learned in the Middle East while studying krav maga. Her head and shoulders went under the man's outstretched arm, and her knee came up on the other side, jamming deep into his midsection with enough force and speed to send him toppling backward as the air whooshed from his lungs.

Moving toward the other man, she nonchalantly kicked the first attacker in the side of his head with her bare foot as he tried to get up. He went sprawling back onto the sand, his body inert.

The first man circled around behind her as she closed on the man who hadn't spoken yet. He was bigger than the other two. He grinned broadly, exposing two gold teeth.

Charity feinted to the left and the man took the bait, grabbing for her. But she was already spinning back the other way, and his arms grabbed nothing but air. She leaped into the air, completing the spin as her right leg whipped out. The bottom of her foot met the man's nose, flattening it and spraying blood everywhere.

He dropped to his knees, his eyes blinking, but his body no longer responding.

Charity finished the spinning back kick, landing lightly in a crouch next to the kneeling man. She grabbed a handful of dreadlocks with her left hand and lifted his head. Then her right fist came down hard on the left hinge of his jaw. The sickening crack left no doubt that he'd be eating through a straw for a while.

Whipping her head around, Charity looked for the first man. When he saw her face, he stopped. That proved to be his undoing, as Victor stepped up behind him and clobbered him with the spent fire extinguisher.

Victor dropped the heavy cylinder and started toward Charity, but stopped in his tracks at the sight of her face.

"Easy now," he cautioned. "They're all down."

She slowly rose from the sand and looked around at the three thugs.

"I knew my first instinct was right about you," Victor said with a grin.

"Your first instinct was that I exhibited poor field craft."

"Okay," he said with a grin, pushing a shock of dark blond hair from his forehead. "My second instinct, then. What the hell was that acrobatic stuff?"

"Staying alive," was Charity's only response.

As she stepped up close to Victor, she glanced toward the man who had been on the receiving end of the thugs' beating. He was struggling to his feet, clutching his side.

Suddenly, the first man Charity had put down jumped to his feet and began scrambling up the hill. In a flash, Charity was after him, screaming like a banshee. The man had a good fifteen-yard head start, but by the time he was halfway up the hill, it looked like a dead heat as to who would reach the road first.

The constant stream of terrifying growls and obscenities from Charity's lips seemed to spur the man on. Above, a car engine started, and the man redoubled his efforts, reaching the top a step ahead of the maniacal woman clawing and charging up the hillside to reach him.

Charity heard a car door slam and the roar of the engine as the car's tires spun sand and loose gravel. Reaching the road, she glared after the receding vehicle, hands on her hips, breathing heavily. A rusty, blue Datsun pickup, more than thirty years old, bounced and weaved up the hill, like a drunk, wheezing boxer.

Charity's shoulders slumped, and she turned to look down on the carnage. Aside from a few planks with blue alcohol flames dancing on them, the fire was out. There wasn't much left of the little Tiki bar.

She'd visited it a couple of times, sat on a stool and looked out over the bay while talking to the little old black man who owned it.

A wave of emotion came over her and she dropped to her knees. She'd done what she'd spent the last year trying so hard to avoid: when her feet had first hit the sand, the lock had opened, and the demons had all flown out.

She usually did that intentionally, when she didn't know just what danger was ahead; the demons kept her focused. This time, she felt that if Victor hadn't stopped her, she would have broken the neck of the man she'd been kneeling over, then calmly walked over and killed the other two.

When the three aggressors were down, there was no longer any danger—but she hadn't intended to unlock the demons the second time.

I can't keep doing this, Charity thought.

And then, without knowing she was speaking, she whispered, "I want to go home."

CHAPTER TWO:

Charity had stashed her gun in the little console of Victor's dinghy before the police arrived. Victor introduced Charity to the little old man, Chet, who had agreed to keep them out of it. Charity and Victor devised a quick timeline of events so their stories would be the same.

When the police arrived, Chet explained that the two men—and another who ran away—had tried to rob him, and they'd burned up his Tiki bar.

"I don't think they knew there were propane tanks inside," he told the lead police officer. He went on to tell him that the propane and liquor bottles had exploded and injured him and his attackers. "These folks arrived in time to put out most of the fire."

"You didn't see where the other man went?" the young policeman asked the three of them. His nametag read *Lucien*.

"He got into an old blue pickup," Charity said, with a touch of a Cuban accent. She pointed up the hill. "It was a Datsun, I think. Then he took off up the hill."

"Mmm," Lucien said, writing in a notebook. "Nothing to worry 'bout. Dis is an isolated incident."

Over his shoulder, Charity couldn't help but notice Chet rolling his eyes at the comment.

"May I see yuh identification?" Lucien asked Victor and Charity.

"Mine's on my boat," Charity said. "We came ashore in kind of a hurry."

"Is dat your dinghy?" he asked, pointing with his chin.

"No," Victor said. "It's mine. She's welcome to use it to go to her boat and get her visa, if that's all right."

"Americans don't need a visa," Lucien said to Victor.

"Well, I don't have a driver's license," Victor said, handing the policeman his own visa. "Don't own a car or a house."

Lucien looked first at Victor, then at Charity. "Go dere and right back, please."

Charity went down to the water's edge and pushed Victor's dinghy into deeper water, then climbed aboard and started the engine. She was glad for Victor's suggestion; it would give her a second to stash her weapon on the *Dancer* before returning.

Officer Lucien seemed suspicious, and though Saint Thomas was an American territory, if either of them were caught with guns here, there would be far too many questions to answer.

Climbing up to the cockpit, she stepped quickly down into the salon, opened the drawer at the nav-station, and put the Sig away in its hiding place. Then she grabbed her passport from the same drawer and returned to the beach.

Lucien had already taken Victor's statement, and now examined Charity's visa. "No house and no car, as well?"

"No," Charity replied. "I have both, but don't bring them with me on the boat. I leave my purse at home as well."

He looked at her sternly for a moment. "Very well, Miss Fleming. Tell me what you saw happen here dis morning."

"I really didn't see much," Charity said. "It was still dark when Mister Cook invited me to breakfast. The explosion happened just as we got into his dinghy. When we got to the beach, he put out what he could with a fire extinguisher and I checked on Chet to see if he was okay."

"Both he and di two men he claimed tried to rob him look like they been fighting."

"Fighting?" Charity said, trying for an incredulous expression. "Look at poor Chet, Officer. Does he look like he could beat those men up? Maybe they were all hit by debris in the explosion."

"Mmm," Officer Lucien said again, as he wrote in his notebook. "Dat was what he said. Di two men and one other put a match to his shack and di liquor blew up, hurting all of them."

Charity looked around at what little was left of Chet's Tiki bar. The sun was well above the horizon now, the sky clear and bright, so nothing was hidden. Charity thought about what the two men would say when they woke up. She doubted they'd be cooperative with the police, and it was also doubtful that they'd admit a woman had beaten them up.

"It was a big explosion," she said. "Good thing there weren't others around. It could have been much worse."

"Mmm," Lucien said again. "Guess yuh right about dat."

An ambulance arrived, and the two men had their vital signs checked before they were put on stretchers and loaded into it. Chet refused treatment, saying he'd only been hit in the side by a board, and felt fine.

Later, after the police and most of the gawkers had left, Victor asked Chet what was really going on. Chet looked from Victor to Charity, then up to a group of people still standing on the road above. Two of them, an elderly island couple that Victor knew, started down the hill.

"Those men have been coming here for a week," Chet explained, his accent a distinct French Creole. "They tell me and other businesses that we need their protection and we should pay them for it."

"Protection?" Victor asked.

"Oi," the tall man approaching said. He was an older man, perhaps sixty, with soft features, skin the color of mahogany, and surprising green eyes. A little round woman with dark skin and light brown eyes accompanied him. "But it is none of your concern, Rene. It is something we must take care of ourselves."

"If I'm here, Henri, it concerns me, too," Victor said. "You are my friends. Please, say hello to another of my friends, Gabriela Fleming." He turned to Charity and said, "This is Mister Henri Heureaux and his wife, Lisette. They own a couple of small rental villas on Peterborg Peninsula."

"My pleasure, Miss Fleming," Henri said.

Charity shook the man's hand, and then his wife's. "I'm inclined to agree with Rene, Mister Heureaux. I'm no stranger to these islands; they're almost like a second home. Those men aren't from around here, are they?"

"No, they are Jamaicans." Henri said it with a bit of venom in his voice. "And please, call me Henri."

"Only if you will call me Gabby," Charity said, liking the old man instantly. "Since when are Jamaican gangs spreading their influence to the Virgin Islands? And soliciting for protection money? That sounds like something from an old noir movie."

Henri smiled at Charity. "There is little to stop the spread of evil here." He then turned to Victor. "But, Rene, my friend, we cannot involve you."

"We're already involved, Henri. Those two men weren't hurt by flying debris, like Chet told the cops."

Henri glanced at Chet, who nodded, then at Charity. Finally his gaze returned to Victor. "When those men wake up, you will be in trouble. All the more reason for you to leave."

"They're not going to say anything to the police," Charity said.

"How can you be sure?"

"It wasn't Rene who beat them up," Charity replied.

Henri gave Victor a confused look, then slowly returned his gaze to Charity and grinned. "Ah, I believe you are right. They won't tell the police who it was that beat them. But there are more of them. Those two will tell the others. And they will come for you. It would be best if you both left the island."

Victor looked at Charity and nodded his head toward the beach. "Can I speak with you a moment?"

They walked away from Henri and the others, and stopped beside Victor's dinghy. "First," he said, "thanks for not spilling my real name."

"And thanks for remembering my alias," Charity said, with a grin. "And giving me a chance to stash my weapon. And, before you say anything else, I'm not leaving."

Victor looked out at their two boats, resting quietly at anchor just off the beach. "Part of me says to pull the hook and set the sails. I don't need the attention."

"Nor do I."

His brow furrowed. "These people are my friends, though. If there's anything I can do to help them, I will. But you're not involved."

"I don't like bullies," Charity said. "I came here to relax and unwind after a mission. I'm staying, and if I can help your friends, I will."

Victor considered Charity's eyes and, for just a moment, he saw that flicker of fire he'd witnessed when she stood over the fallen Jamaican. She looked away and, as she brushed a strand of hair away from her face, he stole a quick glance at her body.

When she looked back at him, he smiled. "You look good. I like the blond hair."

Charity smiled back. "You look good, too. I've missed you."

"Really?" he said, stammering slightly. "On Trinidad, I felt like you couldn't get rid of me quick enough."

"I was working," Charity said, with a shrug. "You were a liability."

It was Victor's turn to stare out over the water. "Yeah, I can see where you're coming from." He looked back at Charity and asked, "So, we're staying?"

"Something's not right here," she replied, turning and slowly walking back toward the group of islanders.

"What do you mean?" Victor asked, joining her.

"Jamaican gangs aren't into extorting protection money. The big money's in drugs and human trafficking." She stopped and turned to him. "How much do these people know about you?"

"I've been here off and on many times," Victor replied. "Usually there are a lot of cruisers here, and most have some work that needs doing and they're not qualified to do it. Same with the locals. I have a decent shop on board. Why take a fishing boat all the way around to Charlotte Amalie, if someone here can do the work? That's who they know me as, a boat worker."

"Then we'll keep it that way for both of us." Charity resumed walking toward the others. "I've been thinking, Henri," she said, as she approached the Heureauxes. "I've been on that boat for months now. Do you have a villa available?"

"A villa?"

"Yes," Charity said. "With a view of the bay?"

"Why, yes," Lisette Heureaux replied, beaming. "The villa on Little Magens Beach is available. It even has a pool and sauna."

"Where is it?"

Lisette pointed to a spot halfway out the long peninsula. "It's there, on the ridge just beyond that small beach."

Where she pointed, Charity could see a house on the highest part of the ridge. Below it was a small, sandy beach. It had a view of the whole bay and the beach they were on. Scanning the ridge and looking up the road from the beach, she could tell that the house had a commanding view of the road, down to Magens Beach and probably more.

"I'll take it," Charity said.

"Well, don't you want to see it first?" the little round woman said.

"Or ask how much?" Henri added.

"I'm sure it'll be roomier than *Wind Dancer*," Charity said.

Lisette cast her eyes down a moment then looked sheepishly at Charity. "It is one thousand dollars a week, I'm afraid."

"Will cash be okay?" Charity asked. "For two weeks?"

Lisette smiled. "Yes, yes, that will be fine. There is one other thing."

"What's that?"

"Well," Henri began, "the sandy beach just this side of the villa is Little Magens Beach. It's known to be clothing optional. It is not permitted, nor sanctioned by either the government or ourselves, but we have no control over what people do."

"I can live with that," Charity said.

They arranged to meet at the villa at noon, so Charity could move and re-anchor the *Dancer* just off Little Magens Beach. Victor and Charity pushed the dinghy out and climbed in, idling slowly out to their boats.

Reaching the *Dancer*, Charity climbed up to the cockpit and turned to look down at Victor. "You're going to move your boat, as well?"

Victor squinted up at her. "Is that an invitation, Miss Fleming?"

"We need to stay close, Victor. Something about this whole thing just seems weird. Who robs a bartender in the morning?" Then she smiled and said, "And as far as anything else goes, let's just take things as they come."

"Yeah, I wondered about that, too," he replied, his boat bobbing in the slight chop, as he held onto *Dancer's* rail. "It would have been smarter to wait until he closed up at the end of the day. Sure, I'll move *Salty Dog* over."

"*Salty Dog*?" Charity asked with a grin. "Not very original, Victor."

"Name she came with," he said, pushing away from the *Dancer*. "Too lazy to change it. Lead the way. I'll anchor upwind of you."

"Off the nude beach," Charity said with a grin. "Figured as much."

She went below and opened the forward hatch over her bunk, leaving the main hatch open, to let the boat air out. She started the engine and activated the electric windlass to pull the anchor. Once it was seated in its roller, she put the transmission into forward and turned the bow to the northwest, following the peninsula.

Little Magens Beach was easy to find. Nearly all the shoreline was craggy rock. A natural jetty of what looked like tumbled down rocks blocked the wave action in one spot about halfway out the peninsula. Over time, sand had built up on the side facing the bay opening, creating a tiny beach area. The cliff above it had been worn down and was lower there, the landscape tangled with palm trees, ferns, cactus, and jagged rocks.

Approaching the house at the far end of the small beach, she zoomed in on the chart plotter. The bottom dropped away from the shoreline very fast. She picked a spot a little past the house and some hundred-and-fifty yards from shore and dropped anchor in forty feet of water. Backing off, she let out three hundred feet of rode and activated the windlass brake until she felt the backward movement stop and the anchor chain rattle. Even if the wind shifted and swung *Wind Dancer's* stern toward shore, she'd have ten feet under her keel, and be about forty or fifty yards from shore.

Satisfied that her ground tackle was secure, Charity shut down the engine. On the foredeck, she released the straps on her tiny dinghy and wrestled it off its cradle and into the water. Minutes later, she had the little outboard mounted, and ran the engine for a moment before climbing back aboard.

In her cabin, Charity packed just a few things in a small backpack. Kneeling by the entertainment center in the salon, she counted down to the ninth CD in the inboard rack and pushed it in. The catch released and she swung the pair of CD racks out, opening them like doors.

Behind the racks was a hiding spot, one of many on *Wind Dancer*. The left side of this one continued several feet deep and contained a long black tactical case, nestled against the hull just below the head. On the right side, two handguns were mounted to the inside of the bulkhead, with boxes of ammo stacked neatly below them on a narrow shelf. On the deck, lay a small black box, which she lifted out and placed on the settee. Opening it, she counted out twenty hundred-dollar bills from a large stack and folded the bills into her back pocket. Then she counted out another hundred dollars in twenties and put that in her other back pocket.

She closed the box and returned it to its hiding place, securing the racks back in place with a click.

At the nav-station, she retrieved her Sig, and stuffed it and the money into her backpack. She closed and latched all the hatches, then climbed up to the cockpit. She secured the main hatch and stepped down into the dinghy. Later, she'd come back out and retrieve a few other things, after checking the house to see what she might need. Between her and Victor, she was sure they had the skills to make any more extortive visits by the Jamaicans a troublesome affair.

Looking over, she saw that Victor was already anchored, and heading toward her in his dinghy. She started the little outboard and pushed away from the *Dancer*, turning toward the north end of the beach and accelerating. Victor changed course and they met at the end of the beach, where a trail wound its way up the rocks, splitting into two separate paths. One led up to the house, and the other angled away to the right, probably up to the road above.

"Tide's nearly full," Victor said, pulling his dinghy up high on the sand and pulling out enough dock line to tie off to a coconut palm. "The dinghies should be safe here and if we need them at low tide, well, it doesn't fall much. We can drag them twenty feet to the water."

Charity secured her dinghy likewise and they each shouldered their small packs and started up the trail. "I'll come back out later and get some more equipment," Charity said. "That pool deck up there should have a good view of the road coming down from the pass."

"What sort of other equipment?"

"I have night vision optics aboard. Also a camera, with a motion alert I can train on the approach road. It will alert me if anyone comes down from the mountains, long before they get to Magens Beach."

"What's your motivation here, Charity?

They reached the split in the trail and Charity stopped and turned around. "What do you mean?"

"You don't know these people," he said, stopping in front of her.

"Let's just say I'm bored," she replied. "And seriously, I don't like bullies."

"Good enough for me," he said, continuing up the trail ahead of her. "It's never boring when you're around."

They reached the top of the cliff, both breathing hard. Charity stopped and turned around. Beneath them, the beach was deserted and the boats looked peaceful, their shadows visible on the sandy bottom.

"Whoa," Victor said. "Even if it was just a thatched hut, the view would be worth the price of admission. Speaking of which, how much do I owe you?"

"Nothing," Charity said, looking away toward Magens Beach. Even from this vantage point, she could tell that most of the road would be visible from some spot on the property. "A rich uncle keeps sending me money."

At the end of the path was a gate, which Victor opened and held for Charity. The gate slammed shut on sprung hinges, and they walked out onto a concrete deck. In the middle was a kidney-shaped pool, with the small, concrete house just beyond. There were five chaise lounges scattered around the deck, plus an umbrella table with four chairs. All the outdoor furnishings were white, with the umbrella a navy blue that matched the throw pillows on the furniture.

The back of the house was nearly all glass. Heavily-tinted windows and French doors spanned the width of the house. One of the French doors swung open as they approached.

Lisette stepped through the door, followed by Henri and Chet. "Welcome to Hilltop," Lisette said, as Charity and Victor walked around the pool and joined them.

Charity stopped and looked all around. Everything, except the mountains looking over the bay, was below them. She could see the whole bay and nearly all of the peninsula road as it wound along the top of the ridge. What was left of Chet's Tiki bar and the burnt palm trees around it could be seen, as well as the road leading up to the switchback high above the far side of Magens Beach. Portions of it could be seen nearly all the way to the pass.

"Would you mind terribly if I ask you something?" Henri said.

"Sure," Victor replied, as Charity turned and looked up at the roof of the house. It appeared to be flat, like most homes built on the islands.

"What exactly do you plan to do?" Henri asked hesitantly. "I mean, about Chet's early morning visitors?"

"How many people have been threatened by this gang?" Charity asked, still looking around at the surroundings.

"Most of the twenty-three homes on the peninsula are rentals," Lisette replied. "We own three. Of the rentals, all but two are owned by local people. All of us, as well as Chet and three other vendors on Magens Beach—people who depend on tourists and beachgoers for their livelihood—have had some negative contact with them."

"Is your place the only one that's been damaged?" she asked Chet

"Yes," he replied. "Until this morning, there have been only taunts and threats, but no violence."

Charity looked at Henri. "My guess is that none of you have paid them anything. Am I right?"

"None that I know of," Henri replied. "But now, I'm not so sure it will stay that way."

"Rene and I have backgrounds in security," Charity said. "Those men are going to come back. They'll demand protection money from you to keep something from happening to your villas, like what happened to Chet's Tiki bar."

"They used Chet as an example," Victor added.

"Again," Henri asked. "What do you plan to do? We cannot allow you to be harmed on our behalf."

"No harm will come to anyone, if it can be avoided," Charity said, then asked all three: "The response time of the police this morning, is that about average?"

They looked at each other.

"I don't know," Henri finally replied. "Today may be the first time the police have been called to this side of the island in an emergency, at least that I can remember."

"So if those guys come back with reinforcements— which they will, and soon—the people here are on their own for more than fifteen minutes? A lot can happen in that short a time."

"I never thought of it that way," Lisette said, frowning. "This has always been a quiet and peaceful place."

"This is a touchy question," Charity said. "Do any of the home or business owners have guns that you know of?"

"You think it will come to that?" Henri asked, pulling his wife close in a protective gesture.

"It may," Charity said. "I was once a Miami police officer, and in the Army before that. The police here might not have the experience, equipment, or manpower to deal with this kind of stuff. In my experience, these things do tend to escalate. So, for at least ten minutes, it's just us."

CHAPTER THREE:

A gray sedan pulled up to a construction gate and stopped. The sign at the entrance read *La Calypso Luxury Resort* and listed the names of the developer, construction management company, and several local investors. The new resort was being built on James Point Beach, on the island of Eleuthera, in the Bahamas.

The engine shut off and the driver's door opened. A man got out of the car and approached the guard shack. He looked to be in his late thirties, fit and professional-looking, wearing pressed khakis and a long-sleeved, pale blue linen shirt.

"Help yuh, sir?" the guard asked, as he opened the door to the small air-conditioned building and stepped outside.

The clean-cut, sandy-haired man removed his sunglasses and took a business card from his shirt pocket. Extending it to the guard, he waited, dark-blue eyes scanning the construction site, which was only in the first stages of development.

Once the guard read the name on the man's card, his eyes came up quickly. "Mistuh Whitaker? Nobody told me yuh was visiting today."

The man looked at the nametag the guard wore. "That's because nobody knew I was coming, Mister Parker," he said with a genuine smile.

Bradley Whitaker was the first name listed on the sign. *La Calypso* would be the seventh high-end, luxury resort that he'd developed and built. Known to be an astute businessman, he made sure his construction projects were always completed on time and on budget. Mostly because he was the kind of man that would, and could, roll up his sleeves and trade his oxfords for boots. Those who worked for him were very loyal and hard-working.

Bradley Whitaker cared about his employees and they shared in his successes.

"Di office trailer is straight ahead, suh," the guard said. "Let me get dis gate open and yuh can go right in."

The guard quickly opened the gate. Having the developer himself visit the construction site was something new. To Kendal Parker, that could mean only one thing: someone was in trouble.

Brad Whitaker got back in his rental car and started the engine. Once the guard had the gate open, he drove through and continued along the rutted road toward several trailers grouped together. A stand of tall pines swayed gently in the breeze beyond the trailers. The taller ones, further from shore, stood ramrod straight, more than a hundred feet tall. Those nearer the shore were twisted and stunted by wind and wave. In the afternoon, they provided shade for the mobile construction offices.

The door to the first trailer opened just as Whitaker stepped out of the car. A man came out, wearing jeans and a blue polo shirt with the Whitaker logo stenciled on the front pocket.

"Mister Whitaker," the man said, extending a beefy right hand as he approached his boss. "I wish I'd known you were coming, I'd have arranged a little better lunch."

"That's okay, Wesley. I had lunch with an investor in town before coming down. Figured that since I was here on the island, I should probably drop by and see how the excavation work was coming along."

"A little behind schedule," the project superintendent replied. He was a big, bald man in his early fifties. *La Calypso* was the third project by Whitaker Developing that he'd overseen, and the fifth that he'd worked on for the company.

"Was the storm bad?" Whitaker asked, shaking his super's hand.

"We had to lay the drag line excavator down for three days because of it, and a few palm trees close to the water came down. But the hole's finished and concrete started two days ago. Care to come inside?"

"Let's walk down to the site, if you don't mind," Whitaker replied. "Three days will be easy for you to gain back."

The two started down a path behind the trailer and soon came to a gaping hole in the ground, several hundred feet across and fifteen feet deep.

"It took the pumps a full day to bring down the water level," Wesley said, pointing toward the center of the massive hole. "We'd factored in two days, so we've already gained back a little time."

"How many rodbusters do you have working down there?" Whitaker asked, his practiced eye measuring the angles and lengths of the shear walls of the concrete foundation yet to be poured. Dozens of men were on the bottom, moving and tying large steel reinforcement rods together, each one raised above the bottom several inches.

"The day crew is thirty men, my six foremen, and their hand-picked laborers," Wesley replied. "I have another crew of five that come in at midnight, to go behind the rodbusters and check the tightness of the fasteners after the steel cools."

"Looks like you'll finish pouring the foundation in a couple of days."

"We could start the columns tomorrow evening, if it weren't so hot. Probably gain back half a day."

"No," Whitaker replied, wiping the sweat from his brow. "Let's not cut any corners just to gain back a half day. Let the steel cool overnight."

"Yes, sir. We can gain some time back by working the next couple of Sundays."

"Just one," Whitaker said. "The men need the down-time. A little delay like this can be made up easy in small chunks, without overworking the crews."

"Yes, sir," Wesley said. "Mind if I ask you something?"

Whitaker put his sunglasses back on and gazed out over the massive pit to the beach beyond. Unlike most places in the Bahamas, Eleuthera's eastern shore faced the open North Atlantic Ocean, sitting right on the edge of the continental shelf. Beyond the beach was nothing but water, all the way to Africa. So, there was nothing to impede or disrupt the wind and waves. The shore was picturesque from this high vantage point. Waves rolled in, meeting the shallows at a near perfect angle to create a long break that lasted nearly two minutes, as the crest met the shore for several uninterrupted miles.

"What's that, Wes?"

"I've known you a long while, and I've worked for a lot of other outfits. You never cut any corners, even little ones, like cooling the steel overnight. A lot of other guys wouldn't even think twice."

Brad looked at his project boss. "When the last cabinet and toilet is set and the construction workers leave for the last time, the job still won't be over."

"What do you mean?"

Brad pointed toward the breaking waves with his chin. "Imagine how big those waves would be if that storm had tracked a few degrees more to the south than it did. If a hurricane like that makes landfall here, I need to know that anyone who is in a building that I put up is safe."

Just then, a car horn began honking in short bursts, then stopped.

"That's my sat-phone," Brad said. "Been expecting a call about a deal on another property. It'll probably start up just after you finish this one." He winked, and they turned back toward the parking area. "I might even be able to give you a few weeks off before material starts arriving."

"Oh, yeah? Thanks, Mister Whitaker. Where's the next one going?"

"The Virgin Islands," Brad replied, stopping beside the rental car, and opening the door. "Meet me at Tippy's at seven. I should be able to tell you more then."

"Yes, sir, Mister Whitaker," Wesley replied.

Brad got in the car and started the engine. Once he was through the gate, he turned south on Queen's Highway, toward Governor's Harbour. He picked up the satellite phone from the console and thumbed to recent calls, tapping the entry for the call he'd just missed.

"I was busy," he said, when the connection was made. "How are things going there?"

Brad listened for a moment, then said, "We have a mutual interest in this deal; you know that. I provide a service to you, and you provide a service to me. I need this deal to go smoothly and soon. One of the parcels I'm interested in is being looked at by another developer."

Brad slowed as he approached the entrance to the small airport. Glancing to the right, he saw his Cessna Citation sitting where he'd left it. The crew had secured the plane and gone into town for the night. They'd be departing just after sunrise to fly to Puerto Rico, where Brad kept one of his yachts. The plane would then fly on ahead and he'd sail the last sixty miles, to have his floating office close by.

Using the boat, he could be close to the land parcels he wanted to buy. Deals like this were better done in person, and he could discreetly visit with each landowner and touch base with the local building department to begin the long application process.

"Look," Whitaker said, switching the phone to his other ear, "the only way I can do anything to assist you is if my projects move forward in a timely manner." He listened to the man on the other end for a moment. "I'll be there in two days. I'd like to meet with amenable sellers when I get there." After another moment, he sighed. "Okay, that can work. But, you'll have to come to Saint Thomas."

He ended the call, then scrolled through his contacts list. He found the number for his captain, Glen, and tapped it, just as he entered the little town of Governor's Harbour.

When Glen answered, Brad said, "Make the boat ready to sail. We leave tomorrow on the afternoon tide." He listened for a moment, then said, "Yes, minimal crew. I hope to wrap up the deal on Saint Thomas in a day or two. The packages will be delivered there in three days."

CHAPTER FOUR:

After Chet and the Heureauxes left, Charity and Victor explored the little villa further. It had two separate suites, one with a large whirlpool tub in the corner. The two walls around the tub were fixed glass panes, affording a fantastic view of the bay. Charity dumped her bag on the bed and opened the French doors onto the huge patio, to let the cool breeze off the water push the stale air out.

"Charity," Victor yelled from the other side of the house. "Come check this out."

She left and crossed the living room to the other bedroom. "Where are you?"

Victor stepped out of the closet. "There's a ladder to a watertight hatch in here."

She squeezed past him into the walk-in closet. The proximity brought back the intimacy they'd shared a year and a half ago, if only for a couple of days.

"Does it open?" she asked looking up at the metal door in the ceiling.

"Don't know," he replied, pulling the ladder down. It telescoped easily and locked into a bracket bolted to the floor. Victor climbed up to the second step and turned the latch, which moved easily. Stepping up further, he pushed the hatch up, opening it on silent hinges. When it locked in place, he climbed further up, using grab rails mounted on the roof.

"Whoa!" he said, climbing the rest of the way up. He turned and looked down. "You gotta see this."

Charity quickly scampered up the ladder, looking all around when she reached the rooftop vantage point. The ladder was in the corner of a large wooden deck, at least twenty feet in both directions. A low rail surrounded it, with the rest of the flat roof extending past the rails. At the opposite corner was an outdoor hot tub. Three more white chaise lounges with matching tables lined a rail, looking toward the southwest.

Walking over to the front corner, Charity could see the road, all the way to where it turned back, up above Magens Beach.

"You can see most of the road all the way to the switchback," Victor said, pointing to the spot at the far end of the beach. There, the road turned back, climbing higher and disappearing at times among the foliage.

"This is perfect," Charity said. "With my camera optics, I can monitor the road easily, maybe further up from the switchback, as well."

Victor leaned against the rail. "You sure you want to get involved in what's going on here?"

"Yeah, why?"

"You ever have any dealings with Jamaican gangs in Miami?" he asked. "Or was that just a part of your cover story?"

Charity turned and faced him, the wind blowing several strands of hair across her face. She pushed it back behind an ear. "No, I really was a Miami cop. They prefer the term *posse* to *gang*. Miami had its share of posses, each as ruthless and violent as the next."

"And you think they'll be back? Seeking retribution?"

"They'll definitely return. And more than just three," she replied, turning back to the road and studying it. "But, not until it gets dark. They prefer early morning and late night raids."

"How do you want to handle it?"

She glanced at the ex-CIA spook. She'd checked out his background when they'd first met, and knew him to have once been a dangerous man. He didn't look the part. Tall, fit, and tanned from days in the sun. Unshaven for several days, hair streaked and disheveled. He looked more like the typical boat bum than a CIA field operative.

"What do you have on board in the way of weapons?" she asked.

"Three handguns and a shotgun," he replied.

"Let's go to your boat first." Charity turned and walked across the deck to the ladder. "We'll grab your guns and ammo, then stop at the *Dancer* and get my equipment."

Minutes later, they came alongside *Salty Dog*, and Victor held the dinghy steady as Charity climbed the boarding ladder. Victor's boat had nearly twice the freeboard of hers. *Wind Dancer* didn't need a ladder; the deck was about hip level when she stood in her dinghy.

Victor climbed quickly to the deck beside her. "There's a small cabinet on the starboard side of the helm," he said, nodding aft and inserting a key in the padlock of the main hatch. "Open that, reach inside and press up on the top."

Charity nodded and went to the helm. Though it was only eleven feet longer than the *Dancer*, Victor's boat looked and felt much larger. Only the small pilothouse extended above the deck, leaving what seemed like acres of foredeck, with wide side decks around the house, and an aft deck large enough for lounge chairs and a table— though there was nothing, just lots of empty deck space, neat and clean. She noticed that while most yachts of this size had beautiful teak or other hardwood decks, *Salty Dog's* decks were all skid-resistant epoxy and fiberglass.

Charity opened the cabinet. Two shelves held rags, mineral oils, and varnish for the brightwork, as well as other assorted gear. Only because she was looking for it did she note that there were several inches of space above the cabinet door to the top of the helm.

Most boats had numerous places to hide things. Ideas for new ones were easy to come up with; then it was just a matter of finding a skilled carpenter. Victor probably had dozens of secret places on board.

She reached inside, pushed against the false underside, and heard a faint click; as she slowly lowered her hand, a hinged panel came down with it. The panel stopped at a forty-five-degree angle, and Charity lifted a heavy object wrapped in oilcloth. Removing the cloth, she found Victor's big Kimber 1911. It was obviously clean and well-oiled. She wrapped the cloth back around it and went to the main hatch, where Victor had disappeared.

"Permission to come below," she called out.

"Yeah," he replied. "Be forewarned, though. It's a mess."

Stepping down into the pilothouse, Charity marveled at the expansive interior. Where the topsides were all functional, the interior was luxurious. The pilothouse had a second helm on the port side, with a comfortable looking captain's chair and a decent view forward and to both sides, through glass windows that surrounded most of the house. A U-shaped dinette was aft the helm. To starboard was the galley, with a full-sized refrigerator and freezer. Except for a chart rolled out on the navigation desk, the pilothouse was immaculate.

"Down here," Victor's voice came from the forward part of the boat.

She followed the sound of his voice down another set of steps into the lower salon. Ahead were two hatches side-by-side, more evidence of a much wider beam than the *Dancer*. The hatch on the left was closed, an engraving of a tall sailing ship carved into the wood. The one on the right was open. She walked through the salon toward it, noting a similar engraving on this hatch.

Victor came out of the forward compartment carrying a Remington twelve-gauge shotgun. "If you look under the couch," he said, handing it to her, "you'll find a folded-up duffel bag. Should be big enough to hide the shotgun."

He disappeared forward again, and Charity laid the Remington across the arms of one of the two barrel-type chairs facing the couch, placing the Kimber on the seat. Then she lifted the seat of the couch, which raised smooth and easy on spring-loaded hinges. She realized it was a gutted hide-a-bed, rebuilt into a storage bin. The couch had been trimmed and reupholstered to fit against the curve of the hull. Apparently, Victor knew—or perhaps was himself—a gifted carpenter.

Victor stepped through the hatch again, carrying two watertight boxes and placed them in the second barrel chair. Charity unfolded the duffle bag and held it open while Victor put the shotgun in, then placed the two boxes inside as well. He unwrapped the Kimber and slid it into a holster inside the back of his shorts, pulling his tee-shirt down over it.

"What's forward?" she asked.

"Day head on the left," he said. "On the right used to be like a Pullman double berth, but I removed it and put in a washer and dryer. The vee-berth I converted into sort of an office."

"May I?" Charity asked, starting that way.

"Knock yourself out," he replied. "But like I said, it's a mess."

Stepping through the hatch, Charity found herself in a short passageway, with a full-sized front-loading washer and dryer to her right. They had a counter above them, with cabinets above that. There was a small pile of laundry in a basket on the counter.

Another hatch opened into what had once been a spacious vee-berth. On the port side, a bookshelf curved forward, following the contour of the hull. Another engraved hatch on the port side led back to a full head, with a shower. To starboard was a desk and a straight-backed wooden chair. Above the desk was a custom-built hutch with glass doors and shelves. The glass was etched with the same nautical design as the hatches.

On the desk was a laptop computer, open to what looked like a Microsoft Word file. She stepped closer and observed that it was some kind of book that Victor was reading. Otherwise, the little office and laundry area were as spotless as the rest of the boat.

Going aft, she caught up with Victor in the pilothouse. "I have one more thing I want to grab," he said, leaning the duffel bag against the dinette. He disappeared down the steps to the salon, and she followed.

A narrow passageway led aft, with a long workbench against the starboard hull and two doors on the opposite bulkhead. Victor went on through and opened yet another engraved hatch at the end of the passageway.

Charity peered after him. In the aft stateroom, she could see a huge bed, with the boat's signature triple aft portholes at the end of it.

"This boat is gorgeous," Charity said, watching as Victor knelt and opened a small cabinet under the bed.

"Nobody built them better than the Chinese in the seventies," he said, smiling up at her.

"Is that a king size bed?"

"Super-king," he replied, standing up with a small box in his hand and a broad grin on his face. "Wanna try it out?"

Taking two steps down into the aft stateroom, Charity pushed the surprised Victor back toward the huge bed and closed the hatch behind her. "Yeah, in fact, I do."

An hour later, having gone to her boat to gather equipment, food, and weapons, Charity and Victor again climbed the path to the little villa.

"Let's lay out the weapons on the table," Victor said, when they got inside. "We can stash some in different rooms, as backup."

"Good idea," Charity said, pulling out a chair and placing her heavy pack on it. "A handgun in each bedroom."

"We're not sharing one?" he asked, with feigned hurt.

Charity opened her pack and smiled seductively at Victor. "I thought we'd share both," she said. "And maybe a few other rooms, too."

It was nearly sunset when they climbed up to the rooftop again. Charity handed her long tactical bag and another backpack up to Victor, then followed him up.

Opening the pack, she began assembling the camera and optics on a short tripod. She zoomed in on a clear spot on the road, well above where it doubled back over Magens Beach, then connected the camera to a small device, using a coiled wire—like an old telephone cord, but smaller.

"What's that?" Victor asked, watching her.

"It's a wireless interface for the camera," she replied. "It can be set to send a signal to a small receiver when there's movement in the camera's viewfinder."

Just then, two motorbikes appeared on the camera's digital display, coming down the hill toward the bend in the road. A red light began flashing on the interface. Charity picked up another device, similar to an old-fashioned pager, and turned it on. It immediately began to emit a low beeping tone. Victor leaned in closer and looked at the camera's digital display. The two motorbikes continued down the road, disappearing from the frame and the beeping stopped.

"Technology has sure evolved in the seven years since I left the agency."

Charity handed Victor a spotting scope. "Watch the bend in the road."

He looked through the powerful little scope. Less than a minute later, the motorbikes slowly came around the sharp turn in the road.

"Perfect choke point," he said. "The alert will give us about a minute of warning."

Charity opened the tactical case and began assembling her M40-A5 rifle. "When they come, I can disable their car. Shoot out the tires and they'll be on foot for the last mile."

"What if they come in more than one car?"

"I have plenty of ammo," she replied, threading the suppressor onto the barrel. "You know how to use that thing?"

Victor examined the scope and looked through it again. "There's a large boulder on the far side of the road at the bend. Range to the boulder is eleven hundred and fifty-eight yards; declination is almost zero. Call it point five degrees." He lowered the scope and looked at Charity. "You can hit a moving target at two-thirds of a mile?"

"If it's moving slow enough," she said, removing a lightweight brown tarp from her pack. In minutes, she had the tarp spread across the equipment. There were dozens of large conch shells all around the rail. She moved several to hold the tarp in place, creating a screen from prying eyes.

The alarm on the little receiver clipped to her belt went off.

"That'll go off a lot," Victor said. "At night, there's very little traffic, though. Too bad you can't program it to recognize a rusty old Datsun pickup."

"If this was a sanctioned mission, I'd have a satellite at my disposal."

"Seriously?" Victor asked, incredulous.

"We've come a long way in fighting terrorists since nine-eleven," she said, and immediately regretted it. Victor's fiancée had been on one of the hijacked planes on that fateful morning seven years ago.

Seeing the concern in her eyes, he said, "Don't worry about it. I've moved on in the last year."

"A new girlfriend?"

"I was living with an island girl on Andros, up until June," he replied, "but I was discovered and had to move fast."

"Did you love her?" Charity asked, sitting on one of the chaise lounges and putting her sunglasses on.

"People like us can't afford emotions," he replied, sitting in the lounge next to her. He stretched out and put his own shades on.

The sun was nearing the mountains on the other side of the bay. Charity reclined in her chair and watched it sink lower and lower. It was always around sunset that she thought about her friends and former co-workers. Her friend Jesse often said that the end of the day was a time to reflect on what had been accomplished.

She'd had many long strings of days where she'd accomplished very little. Lately, she'd even been having trouble finding value in her accomplished missions.

"Why are you still doing this?" Victor asked, as if reading her thoughts.

She removed her sunglasses, turned her head, and smiled. "Doing what?"

"You know what I'm talking about," he said.

Charity leaned back again, closing her eyes and feeling the sun full on her face. "I've been wondering that myself."

"What would happen if you just up and left?"

"I don't know," she replied. "What? You want me to go on the run with you now?"

"The thought has crossed my mind," he replied, turning his head and grinning at her. "Especially since running into you this morning."

Charity sat up and turned toward Victor. "Why don't you come in? I bet my handler could find a place for you in DHS, and call off the Agency at the same time."

"No way," he replied, sitting forward and sweeping his arm toward the view before them. "Give this up? I spend my nights beneath a thousand island stars. Give up that feeling when a strange wind snaps at my sails? The spray on my face of an ocean I've never tasted before? A sunset like this from a new place every day?"

"It's become more than just a means of escape, hasn't it? The sailing lifestyle, I mean."

"Yeah," he replied, sighing wistfully. "A lot more."

"I know the feeling."

The pager on Charity's belt beeped again. She quickly brought the spotting scope up and looked toward the road. Several people on bicycles were pedaling hard, heading up toward the pass. She panned the beach and the buildings along it. She easily spotted the motorbike couple; they were the only ones still on the beach. Most of the small businesses that catered to tourists were closing up.

"This time of year," Victor began, "there aren't very many tourists here. As soon as the sun goes down, the road will be practically desolate."

The sun, in a magnificent display of color, slowly slipped below the mountains across the bay. It was completely dark in a matter of minutes. A small lamp on the corner of the rail by the hot tub came on.

"I'll go down and get some food cooking," Victor offered.

"I put two steaks in the refrigerator," Charity said. "We'll have to go into town tomorrow to reprovision."

Alone on the rooftop, she gazed up at the stars. Far in the distance, she heard two engines start, and a pair of lights jerked and bumped unsteadily across the sand down on Magens Beach.

The couple on the motorbikes, Charity thought. A few minutes later, she could see them driving up the road toward the bend. Her pager began beeping as the couple drove past the spot in the road on which the camera was trained.

Relaxing, Charity looked up at the stars again. The moon hadn't yet risen; with very little ambient light to dilute the sky, the light of a billion stars sparkled in her eyes.

Why the hell am I *doing this?* she wondered. Her last mission had been completed only a week ago, and the two weeks it had taken had sapped her, both physically and emotionally. What she needed was down time, alone time. Time away from any and all people. That was how she decompressed.

Later, there would be time to mingle among civilized society. But, right now, Charity knew that her nerves were like a ticking time bomb. She'd been second-guessing her career change quite a lot over the last few months.

"Why *not* run off?" she said aloud, coming to a decision. She would contact the director as soon as things were finished here. She'd leave and go home, or resign. Or do like Victor, and just sail away.

Whatever it took.

Crap! Charity thought, suddenly realizing that she hadn't checked her messages in hours. Though she didn't like turning her phone on, her laptop was downstairs and she couldn't leave the roof. She retrieved her phone from her purse, powered it on, and opened the mail app.

"Of all times," she said aloud, seeing the one saved message in her draft folder.

Then she opened it, and her mind went in several directions at once.

Half an hour later, Victor returned. "Everything quiet up here?" he asked, sliding a tray onto the deck, before climbing up.

Not inside my skull, Charity thought.

"Yeah," she replied, turning her phone off and putting it away. "The couple on the motorbikes left a few minutes ago. Is it always so quiet here?"

"Yeah," he replied, placing the tray on the small table between the two lounge chairs. "One of the reasons I love this place. Everything on this side of the island closes just after sunset. During tourist season, there's usually still people on the beach at night, lighting bonfires, playing guitars, singing, and drinking. But this time of year, not so much."

He sat down on the other lounge and lifted the top from the tray, setting it aside. Two plates were beneath it, each with a perfectly browned ribeye and a large potato. "Hope you like your steak kinda rare. You didn't say."

The smell reminded Charity how hungry she was. They'd been on the go, and she hadn't eaten since very early in the day. "Knock the horns off and warm it up, my dad always said."

"My kinda guy," Victor said, cutting a piece of steak and putting it in his mouth.

"You remind me a little of him. Yeah, you two would probably have gotten along. He loved sailing. His brother owned a boat exactly like *Wind Dancer*, and the three of us sailed every weekend and all summer long."

"When did you lose him?" Victor asked, chewing thoughtfully.

"The same day you lost your fiancée," she replied.

Victor stopped chewing and looked at Charity's profile a moment in the moonlight. She didn't elaborate, and he didn't ask. They ate quickly with little more talking, leaving not a crumb on either plate.

Charity sat back and yawned. Her hunger sated for now, she realized that she'd been going for nearly twenty-four hours.

"How do you want to do this?" Victor asked. "You're exhausted."

"I noticed two sleeping bags in that closet below," she said, getting up from the chair. "I'll get the dishes and bring them up. We can sleep under the stars."

"You're that sure they'll come tonight?"

Just then the beeper went off, and they both looked up toward the road. A car was moving slowly down the hill. Charity brought the spotting scope up, switched the night vision optics on, and looked through it. The image was sharp, the same gray-green as her rifle scope.

"That's them," she said. "Same Datsun pickup. Four men in the back."

She handed the scope to Victor and scrambled to the nest, where her rifle and camera were set up. Lying prone, she turned on the rifle's optics and chambered a round, bringing the stock into her shoulder.

"Watch them, and let me know when they're near the curve," she instructed Victor.

He already had the spotting scope trained on the pickup as it slowly descended the hill. "They just turned their lights off," he said. "They're coming very slowly."

"Perfect," Charity whispered, pressing her cheek into the stock. Had they left their lights on, she'd have had to take the shot just as they came into the curve, the headlights on the truck would have made it impossible to even see the tires through the night vision optics.

The seconds seemed like hours as Charity stared through the scope.

"Just a few yards to the turn," Victor whispered.

Charity watched through the gray-green optics as the vehicle appeared from behind some trees and slowed even more for the sharp turn. In less than a second, her practiced eye registered that the men in the back all carried weapons of some kind—baseball bats and crowbars. She didn't see any guns.

Slowly, she took the slack out of the trigger and moved the reticles to a spot where she judged the truck's right front tire would be in one-and-a-half seconds.

The rifle recoiled, making a cracking sound no louder than an arrow hitting a target. The truck lurched for a second as she brought the scope back on target. It stopped and the men all got out.

Charity ejected the spent cartridge, chambering another round.

"Nailed it!" Victor said, excited, but his voice subdued.

Together, they watched. The men in the truck seemed to be arguing. One pointed at the flat tire, then pointed down the road toward the beach. The men returned to the truck and got in.

"They're gonna drive on the flat," Victor said.

Sure enough, the truck slowly started moving down the hill. Charity brought the stock up tighter to her cheek and shoulder. She placed the crosshairs on the bottom of the left front tire and squeezed the trigger.

Again, the rifle bucked. In the second and a half it took for the round to reach it, the tire had rolled forward just enough, and the bullet blew a hole in the other front tire. Again, the truck lurched and stopped. Charity quickly chambered another round, moved the scope to the only other tire she could see—the right rear—and fired again.

"Well," Victor said, "they're not going anywhere now."

The men got out of the truck, several walking all the way around it, pointing at the other flat tires and searching on the road behind the truck.

"Looks like they think they ran over some busted glass or something," Victor said.

The air was calm, not a breath of wind moving the tall palm trees, either around the house or on the road. One man went to the truck and after a moment came back with a rifle, which he held like a cane, the butt on the road.

Aiming carefully, Charity took a slow breath and let it out while taking up the slack in the trigger. The rifle bucked a fourth time, and the stock of man's rifle splintered. He dropped it and ran for the back of the truck. The others took cover there a second later.

"Dayum," Victor said, drawing the word out. "Remind me never to piss you off."

"What do you think they'll do now?" Charity asked.

"I can only go on what I think *I'd* do. I'd leave and come back with more guns."

As Charity watched the truck, one of the men darted from around the passenger side, taking cover behind a palm tree downhill from where the truck sat.

"You see that guy?" Victor asked, as a second man ran past the man that Charity was watching.

"I got the first one," she said, aiming her rifle. "Keep an eye on the second guy."

"He's behind a big boulder, ten feet past the first one."

Charity fired, hitting the palm tree dead center. She quickly moved her sights down the road, looking for a big boulder. Finding it, she saw the man crouched behind it. He was shouting back toward the others. She aimed at a spot on the rock that would ricochet the bullet up and to the right, and fired once more.

The man bolted back toward the truck, just as the sound of the bullet careening away from the rock reached Charity's ears. She followed him with the scope and saw the first man running ahead of him.

"That ricochet will let them know it's a gun for sure," Victor said. "And that we can see in the dark."

"Now they know the night isn't their friend," Charity said.

They watched as, one by one, the men ran up the hill. Each one stopped and ducked behind whatever rocks or trees provided cover. In a few minutes, they were gone over the high pass, leaving their beat-up truck in the road.

"They'll go off and lick their wounds now," Victor said. "After some rum and ganja, they'll come back. With guns."

Rising from her nest, Charity stood at the rail beside Victor. "Not for a few hours, at least. We can both get some sleep."

Victor looked at her and smiled. "I'll get the sleeping bags."

CHAPTER FIVE:

Walking a desolate road, at night and in a strange land, wasn't something Claude Whyte enjoyed. Getting shot at by an unseen person, he liked even less. When he and his posse reached the pass, they stopped to rest a moment. A spliff was produced, lit, and passed around.

"How dey able to see in di dark?" one of Whyte's men said.

"And to shoot like dat?" another said, "Wit no noise? Dey hadda be really close, mon. And using a silencer."

"What I and I wanna know, mon," Claude said, looking around at each of his men in the light of the rising moon. "How dey know we was coming?" he growled, punctuating each word with a menacing scowl.

Whyte's second in charge, a vicious man named Tarone McFarlane, looked around the group before taking a long drag on the spliff and passing it to Claude. "Dat a good question, mon. Maybe one a dese half eediats have a loose tongue in di wrong place."

Suddenly, the other four men in the group became nervous. The first to speak, a skinny youngster called Chris Henry said, "Dey had to find out some udda way, Busha. Yuh didn't even tell *us* where we was going."

Claude thought about that a moment. The young man was right. Only he and Tarone had spoken to Jacob, the only man to return with the driver, earlier in the day. He'd been beaten up pretty bad. The other two were in the hospital, with a policeman outside their door. Jacob had told him that the group was jumped by several people, after torching the old man's shack. But the way he'd said it had made Claude doubt his words.

"Something is going on heah dat we don't know 'bout," Claude said, studying his second man. He and Tarone had been together for many years. Could this man he'd called friend since childhood be the one that had told these islanders that they were coming? "Let's get back to di yard."

"It duppy, mon," another man mumbled, as they slowly trudged down the road.

Tarone shoved the man who spoke, causing him to stumble and nearly fall into the dirt on the side of the road. "Ain't no duppy, yuh rum head! Dat was a flesh and blood person shooting dat gun."

"Whatever it was," Claude said, getting more incensed with every step. "It gwon die. And di mon gonna have to raise di price for di killin'."

"Whut we do now, Busha?" Tarone asked his boss.

"We get di guns, mon."

It was another mile to the house they'd been staying in on the other side of the hills. And with every step, Claude wondered where he'd gone wrong, and whom he could trust.

CHAPTER SIX:

Still breathing hard, with her heart pounding in her chest, Charity rolled off Victor's body onto her back, staring up at the stars. Her breathing slowed, and soon her heart rate came under control as she lost herself in the vastness of the night sky. It always made her feel very small, like all her worries and struggle didn't really amount to anything at all in the grand scheme of the universe.

She suddenly remembered the message from Stockwell: *Stand down. Return to Homestead at earliest. It is over.*

The message had a time stamp that showed it was saved earlier in the afternoon. Just after she and Victor had made love on his boat, then loaded her gear into his dinghy.

A chill came over her suddenly. *Was he watching from a satellite?*

Her naked body went suddenly rigid at the thought. How else would he know that she and Victor were involved in the incident this morning? *Why else would he order me to stand down?*

"We need to go inside," Charity said, suddenly rising, and pulling her tee-shirt on.

"Huh?" Victor said, lying on his back spread-eagled.

Charity leaned in close to his ear. "Someone might be watching us." She pulled her jeans on, wiggling them over her hips. "Come on, Victor."

What she said must have taken a second for him to process, but then he was up and pulling on his shorts. "Where?"

"I'll tell you in a minute."

Once they were down from the roof, Charity went quickly into Victor's bathroom. It had a huge shower, closed in with thick glass blocks from floor to ceiling. The glass wall curved around, overlapping a second curved, glass wall, with several feet between the two, serving as the shower's entrance. There was no door.

"What the hell are you—" Victor started to say.

Charity wheeled and put a finger to Victor's lips. Then she reached into the shower and turned the water on full blast. Quickly, she stripped out of her clothes, tossing them on the bed in the next room.

Victor caught on to what she was doing and stripped down also, then Charity led him into the hot, steamy shower. They leaned against the far wall, facing each other, water cascading down the sides of their bodies from the overhead rain jets.

"What's going on?" Victor whispered.

"I got a message from my handler earlier today, telling me to stand down and return immediately to Homestead. He said *it's over.*"

Victor thought about that for a moment. "Stand down from what?"

"That's just it," she replied, her voice low. "The message was sent while we were loading equipment from my boat to your dinghy. I only checked it just before those men came."

"I don't get it," he said. "How does the message equate to someone watching us up there on the roof?"

Charity pointed upward. "Eye in the sky."

"So you think your handler is keeping tabs on you from space? And your equipment's bugged?"

"Nothing's beyond his capabilities," she replied. "His team has a satellite devoted to their use."

"What about your other missions?" he asked. "Have you been marginally successful?"

"Completely successful," she replied, a bit too loud and a shade indignant.

Victor looked down into Charity's eyes. "You know things."

"No," she said. "They wouldn't—"

"You thought they were watching us just now," he interrupted. "They've tried to kill me four times now. What did you say in your reply?"

"I haven't replied yet. Things began happening really fast."

"Good," he said. "Hold off on doing that. We can sleep on it."

"What about these people here?" Charity asked. "We stopped those guys once, but they'll be back. If I'm being watched and ignore orders, there'll be hell to pay."

"They won't be back tonight," Victor said. "Besides, if they are watching and the message was sent earlier today, you not only ignored orders, but opened fire on civilians. But if it makes you feel better—and I know it would me—we can camp out on the roof like you said. What's your handler gonna do, kill you twice when you go back?"

"He's not going to do that," Charity said. But, the truth was, a small tingling in the lizard part of her brain, that part that dealt strictly with survival and self-preservation at any cost, was already pushing into her conscious mind.

Nothing's beyond his capabilities.

"Let's get dressed and get back up there," she said. "Someone I know was once able to spot a satellite. But we can't talk."

"How do you...?" he began, then remembered why they were in the shower. "I have something in my pack, an RF detector."

"You have a radio frequency detector, and we're naked and whispering in this shower?"

Victor looked down the length of her, taking in the ripe fullness of her breasts, the flat, tanned belly, and the swell of her hips. "You really didn't give me much of a chance," he said, grinning lewdly.

"Don't tell me you're one of those guys who gets aroused at danger."

He shrugged, moving closer. "When in a Roman tub...."

"It's a shower, Vic. Not a Roman tub." She pushed him away. "Go get your toy and we'll check everything in my room first."

Turning off the shower, Charity padded naked through the room. Victor admired her retreating form as he followed. She left the room and he picked up his pack from the floor, tossing it on the bed.

Charity went straight through the connecting room to her bedroom. She opened her pack and dumped the contents on the bed, spreading everything around. Hurriedly, she slid on a pair of clean panties, cargo shorts, and a tank top, just as Victor entered.

He'd taken the time to put on a pair of shorts and a tee-shirt, and he held a small device in his hand—whatever he had retrieved from his stateroom before she'd jumped him. With a finger to his lips, he approached and began passing the device over her things. He looked at her and shook his head, then looked all around the room.

Charity pointed upward. "All my other gear is up there."

They walked together back to Victor's closet and climbed back up to the roof. Nearly everything was under the tarp, so she grabbed the pack she'd brought her gear up in and tossed it under the tarp, as well.

Charity slid one of the lounge chairs over, grabbed another big conch shell and tied the loose corner of the tarp to it, laying the conch over the back of the chair. The tarp stretched ten feet from the two rails, creating sort of a tent.

They both dropped to their hands and knees and crawled under the makeshift blind. One by one, Victor scanned all of Charity's equipment, even going as far as to activate all the optics and recheck them.

"You're clean," he said. "I wouldn't say the same for your boat and laptop, though. They both probably have at least a location finder."

"That's a relief," Charity said, dragging the two sleeping bags under the tarp with them. "Help me stretch these out. We need to lay on our backs, with our heads outside the tarp."

"To look for a satellite?"

"Yeah," she said. "Indulge me."

In minutes, they were both staring up at the night sky, only their heads exposed outside the tarp. "All I see is stars," Victor said. "Sure, some are probably planets, I'm no celestial expert. But how do you see a satellite?"

"It's simple," Charity said. "I was told that this guy stared up at the stars for quite a while. Knowing that a surveillance satellite was probably going to be right overhead, he discounted all but those stars within a few degrees of arc above him. Stars move—or rather, the Earth rotates—"

"And a surveillance satellite would be in geosynchronous orbit and wouldn't appear to move."

"Exactly," Charity said. "Glad to know you're not just a pretty face and a hard body."

"Isn't the guy supposed to say that?" Victor said. "Only one flaw in your friend's theory. It's almost midnight and a satellite directly over our heads would be in the shadow of the Earth. Or do they have lights, like planes?"

"Hmm, you're right. Now that you mention it, I heard that he did it just before dawn."

"So, what do we do until dawn?" Victor asked, taking Charity's hand in his.

She looked over at Victor and smiled at his profile. The moon was just rising, casting eerie shadows around the landscape below. Victor turned toward her and they gazed into one another's eyes. Charity reached over and pulled him on top of her. Taking his face in both hands, she kissed him passionately.

Later, they fell asleep, his arm around her and her head on his shoulder. They slept soundly until the alarm on Charity's wristwatch began to beep.

Still tired, she started to rise, but only made it halfway to a sitting position, when her face met the sagging tarp. She dropped back onto her side and shook Victor's shoulder.

"The sun will be up in less than an hour," she said. "We need to see if we can spot that satellite."

Victor's eyes barely opened. "Woman," he moaned, "you've sapped me of every ounce of energy I ever thought I had."

"Come on," she said, wrestling his legs out of the way. "We need to align ourselves to the poles."

"I'm pretty sure you caused the poles to *shift* last night," Victor said, lifting his legs, and turning his body alongside hers.

"Concentrate," she said. "He's an early riser and will be expecting a response."

Victor yawned and rubbed the grit of sleep from his eyes, then stared up into the pre-dawn sky. Minutes passed and they chatted about innocuous subjects, without taking their eyes off the stars. Finally, after an hour, they both agreed that every visible object in the night sky was moving.

"Who the hell is this guy who can see satellites?" Victor asked.

"He used to train snipers. Just before I started doing what I'm doing now, some really sick people captured him. But he escaped, and not only did he find the satellite being used to monitor the search for him, he signaled it with a laser bore sight. His name's Jesse McDermitt."

Victor tensed. After a moment, he rolled onto his side and looked at her. Charity tore her eyes away from the sky, satisfied that there was no spy satellite looking down on them. So how did Stockwell know?

She looked at Victor. His face was barely visible.

"Something wrong?" she asked.

"This McDermitt guy," Victor said. "About my size? Former Marine with DHS now?"

"You know him?" she asked.

"He's the reason I had to bug out of the Bahamas last June."

"I doubt he was after you," Charity said, dismissing it immediately.

"Why's that?"

"You lived," she replied. "If he had his sights on you, you'd be dead. He's reputed to have been one of the best there ever was."

"Still seems a little weird," Victor said. "He did tell me that he wasn't after me, but I didn't want to take any chances. He and some other guys seemed to have been on some kind of rescue mission and things went wonky."

"Well, if he said he wasn't, he wasn't." Charity rolled on her side to face Victor. "I've been thinking about what you said and how you have to live your life. Yeah, I know things now that our leaders would rather nobody ever hear about. If my handler wasn't talking about what we're doing here, what was he talking about?"

"What exactly did the message say?"

"*Stand down*," Charity recited, quoting the email. "*Return to Homestead at earliest. It is over.*"

"If he wasn't talking about what we're doing here, he must be talking about your job in general."

"My job?"

Victor arched an eyebrow. "You work for a government that transitions power every four to eight years."

"Politics wouldn't have anything to do with it. We're at war."

"America's military is at war," Victor said, frowning. "America's at the mall."

"You really think that might be all there is? Getting the dirty laundry all safely hidden before the new boss arrives?"

"Wouldn't be the first time. One of my early mentors at the Agency was around back in the seventies. There were a lot of people moved around just before Nixon resigned, and again before Carter took office."

With the sun just beginning to tinge the eastern sky, Charity took her phone out. "So, how should I reply?"

"What do you *want* to do?"

Charity thought about it. She loved the time she had to herself between missions, and loved sailing *Wind Dancer* to new places. It was the missions she'd grown to dislike.

The idea of fighting terrorists by their own rules had fueled her, but aside from the first one, it had been like she was being sent around the Caribbean to clean up messes that had nothing to do with fighting the enemy, or national security. If she went back and everything was fine, they might move her, like Victor said, maybe take the *Dancer* back. Perhaps even destroy her.

She seriously doubted she'd be in a situation like Victor's, though. She knew Stockwell was a soldier more than anything else, not a spook. An officer is apolitical and will follow lawful orders. But, a soldier is also charged with the duty and responsibility to disobey an unlawful order. If Stockwell were ordered to eliminate her, Charity felt almost certain that was an order he'd disobey. Or would he?

She powered the phone up and accessed her email. After erasing the message from Stockwell, she composed a short response.

Only she and Stockwell had access to the mail server, and no messages were ever actually sent, just saved as a draft. This avoided any kind of paper trail, electronic or otherwise. That thought gave her pause, as her finger hovered over the save button. Their method of communication left no loose ends.

She made a quick change to the message, saved it, and turned the phone back off.

"What'd you tell him?" Victor asked.

"I just delayed it."

Victor went down to make breakfast. They'd decided early on that he was the better cook. They ate in silence, occasionally looking out toward the beach at the end of the bay. Everything was quiet there, and the bay still empty.

They talked, diverting their attention from what they were doing and what might happen. They'd both been in surveillance situations before. It could be very monotonous, and you needed the diversions. At night, it was even more important. Diversions kept you awake and alert when shadows hid everything from sight. During the day, diversions were easier. Naming cloud shapes, watching for dolphins, talk of far-away places they've been and others they'd like to see, changes and upgrades they'd done or wanted to do on their boats

"There are some other things I need from my boat," Charity said. "I'll go out this afternoon and get them."

"What kind of other things?" Victor asked.

"Since they know we can see them coming down the road, they'll probably stop at the pass and come down on foot, off the road."

"Makes sense," Victor agreed. "You have something else that'll stop them on foot."

"Well, yeah," Charity replied. "But, we won't resort to explosives except as a last resort." She pointed up to the rough terrain between where the higher part of the road switched back and the lower part of it. "What I had in mind was going up the road there and setting some motion sensors in the woods."

"Then do the same as last night? Run them off with some well-placed near-misses?"

"Exactly," Charity said.

By afternoon, they'd grown bored with watching the road, and turned to watching a monstrous motor yacht that had just entered Magens Bay. It was at least a hundred feet long and had several decks, all shiny white and dark glass, on the blue water.

"Way more money than brains," Victor said, as the behemoth dropped a massive anchor about a hundred yards beyond their boats.

Charity rose and put her sunglasses on. "I'll be back," she said. "We need to get those motion sensors in place before dark."

She was back in less than half an hour, and they set off up the road. Halfway to the switchback, they split up, scrambling and pulling their way up the steep hill twenty yards apart. They activated the sensors, attaching them to half a dozen random trees halfway up the easiest part of the incline.

"We never did get into town for provisions," Victor said, when they were back at the house. "I have some mahi I caught before getting here. It's in the freezer, though."

"Go ahead and start the potatoes," Charity said, watching a launch leave the huge yacht with four people on board. "I have chicken in the fridge on the *Dancer*. Your fish won't thaw in time. They'll wait until it's dark, and it'll take them a long time to get down that hill."

Again, Charity took her little dinghy out to the *Dancer* and climbed aboard. Putting the chicken in a plastic bag, she stuffed it into her pack, then went back on deck and dropped it into the dinghy before untying the painter.

Before stepping down, she looked at the huge ship anchored off her stern, casting a shadow from the setting sun over the *Dancer*. A man crossed the aft deck and sat down in a chair.

CHAPTER SEVEN:

Sixteen hundred miles away, a broad-shouldered man with a square jaw and crew cut sat ramrod-straight in a functional and sturdy executive chair. The chair was in the outer office of the Homeland Security Secretary. Though he was precisely on time for the appointment, the man had been waiting for ten minutes.

As a former Army airborne officer, waiting came second nature to him. Waiting, and being ready for anything.

"Would you like a cup of coffee, Director?" the office manager asked. She was new.

The man was no stranger to this office. His official title was Associate Deputy Director of Homeland Security, Caribbean Counter-terrorism Command.

It was a mouthful, and most people in DC just called him Colonel.

"No, thanks, ma'am," Travis Stockwell replied, with a curt nod and a slight lift to the corner of his mouth.

It was as close to a smile as he could muster. Stockwell was no stranger to politics either, and he could read the writing on the wall. She was new, but hadn't offered her name. A major election was coming in less than two months. The conventions had just ended, and the nominees were selected. The city was abuzz with excitement.

And just as soon as this one was over, the buzz will begin to build for the next election—a never-ending cycle. It was a wonder any work at all was ever accomplished here.

Though their work was vital, Stockwell knew that both of the candidates vying to become the leader of the free world would move quickly to cut back on—and possibly eliminate—his position and his team as soon as they were in office.

But Stockwell was an Army officer. Throughout his long career, his mantra had always been to have a back-up plan for every contingency. He was a proactive officer; regardless of the political ramifications of the coming election, he already had a plan in place for his people.

The phone on the desk buzzed and the new office manager picked it up and listened for a moment. "Yes, sir," she said and hung up the receiver. "The secretary will see you now, Director."

He nodded once more and strode to the door, which opened as he approached. "Come in Travis," Secretary Chertoff said, extending his hand. Stockwell shook it and followed him into the inner office.

Behind her desk, the office manager slowly shook her head and turned back to her computer screen.

An hour later, Stockwell was on the Beltway. He stopped at his townhouse outside of Potomac, Maryland and was back on the road in ten minutes. Even with traffic, he managed to make it to Dulles International Airport less than an hour after leaving Chertoff's office.

He parked at the private aviation terminal and went inside. The attendant at the counter told him his plane was warming up and he could board immediately. Minutes later, they were wheels-up and heading south.

"Make yourself comfortable, Colonel," the steward told him, coming through the door to the flight deck. "We'll arrive at NAS Boca Chica in less than three hours. Can I get you something?"

Stockwell searched his memory for the man's name, as he unbuckled the seat belt. "Thanks, Burt. It's early, but I could sure use a drink."

"Yes, sir," Burt replied. "Glenfiddich?"

"Thanks. And can you give me two minutes on the secure phone?"

"Yes, sir," Burt replied and went to the aft cabin, pulling a small accordion door closed.

Stockwell went forward and sat down on a small sofa. A white telephone with no buttons sat on the table next to it. When he picked up the receiver, an operator answered almost immediately. He gave her his name and security code, and the name of the person he wanted to talk to.

A moment later, a familiar voice answered.

"Travis here," Stockwell said. "I'll be down there tonight. Staying at Boca Chica. I need to talk to you face-to-face in the morning."

He listened for a moment and said, "Perfect, I'll join you. It concerns him, too. What time are you leaving to go up there?" After a moment, he replied, "Okay, I'll be there at oh-six-hundred."

He hung up the phone and returned to his seat, placing his briefcase on the coffee table. Burt returned with his drink, then went up to the flight deck, leaving Stockwell to his work.

When they touched down at the Naval Air Station just outside Key West, Travis put on his jacket, even though he knew it was going to be hot and humid when they opened the door. The jacket concealed his sidearm. He picked up his briefcase and go-bag, and went down the steps into the sultry, tropical air.

A car pulled up alongside the airplane, and Stockwell got in the backseat. Without a word, the driver pulled away and drove the short distance to the visiting VIP quarters. Stockwell waved off the offer of help with his bags and went inside. He was informed that his room was ready, and minutes later he dumped his go-bag on the bed. Tossing his briefcase next to it, he opened it, took his laptop to the desk, and plugged it in to charge.

Turning it on, Travis found he had no new communications that couldn't wait. He composed a short message and saved it in the draft file. Then he sent a quick message to the base motor pool, requesting a car for the morning. He ordered room service, grabbed a quick shower before his meal arrived, and dressed for bed. When the food arrived, he ate without tasting it, then stretched out on the big bed. He would need to wake early to make his destination on time.

The next morning, before the sun had risen, Travis turned into a familiar driveway forty miles up the island chain. It had only been a little over half a day since he'd received his orders and left the hustle and bustle of the nation's capital. But here, it was like he'd been swept up in some sort of quantum whirlpool and deposited in another era.

The driveway wound through overhanging tropical trees, then opened onto a small crushed shell parking area. Beyond it sat a low, wooden structure with a metal roof and windows along three sides, nearly all of them opened to the warm breeze. There was no sign to indicate what sort of business it was.

Travis knew what it was.

Parking the car, he got out and took a deep breath. The air was thick with moisture that would stick right to your skin. A light breeze came off the water, carrying the low-tide scent of salt and iodine. It mixed with the exotic scents of the wild-growing tropical trees, bushes, and flowers.

Travis felt a calm come over him, like he'd returned to a safe and familiar place after a long period of chaos. Leaving his bag in the car, he walked to the door of the establishment and went inside, carrying only a large, thickly stuffed envelope. More scents assaulted his nostrils: kitchen odors, heavy with spices and the scent of frying bacon and sausage. He was hungry, and knew just what would sate that hunger.

"Heard you was coming," the portly, bearded man behind the bar said. "How ya been?"

The *Rusty Anchor* was empty. But Travis could hear voices from outside on the deck. Taking a seat at the combination liquor and breakfast bar, he reached across and shook the man's hand. "Glad to be out of the city, Rusty, even if only for a little while. How are things here in paradise?"

Rusty Thurman was a Conch. His family had home-steaded this land generations before. He was short and big around the middle, with a bald head and thick red beard, starting to gray at the corners of his mouth. Travis knew that a powerful and capable former Marine lurked beneath the weak-looking exterior.

"Fair to middling," Rusty said. "You gonna have some breakfast?"

"My mouth's been watering since I left the air station. Any janga?"

Rusty smiled. "How ya want it?"

"How about a couple of big breakfast tacos?"

"I'll let Rufus know," the bar owner replied and went out the back door.

Just then, the other door opened. Travis turned toward it.

"How are you, Director?" Rusty's daughter, Julie, asked. She was married to Stockwell's second-in-command and had joined his team out of the Coast Guard's Maritime Enforcement. "Deuce said that was probably your car. He's putting some things on the boat."

"I hear congratulations are in order," Travis said, giving the young woman a quick hug.

"Yes, sir," she replied. "It's a boy."

She sat down at the bar as the door opened again and Deuce Livingston stepped inside. A tall, powerfully built man with Nordic features, he smiled at his boss. They shook hands and exchanged pleasantries.

"The man's not going to like this," Deuce said, sitting down next to his wife.

"I have some paperwork to do for Dad," Julie said, leaving them alone at the bar and going behind it to the office.

"I may have some good news for him." Travis slid the envelope toward Deuce. "In there is all the paperwork you'll need. Just give that to Miss Koshinski and she'll know what to do with it."

Deuce unbent the clasp on the envelope and opened it, thumbing the pages it contained. Letters of recommendation from high government officials, business filings in triplicate, licenses, documentation, and other legal papers.

"Thanks, Director," Deuce said. "It means a lot."

"Yeah, well, if our meeting this morning doesn't go well, I might be coming to you for a job."

"So, it's all going away?" Deuce asked. "Even your position?"

"Has to. Plausible deniability and all that crap. America can't have federal police agencies, no matter the intent. We were wrong to move things in that direction." Travis paused and glanced into the office at Julie, before continuing. "So, yeah, it's all going away, Deuce. The new administration, regardless of the election's outcome, is going to let us go, claiming budget cuts or this or that, leaving our people no time to look for other means of earning a living. I met with the secretary yesterday and he introduced me to the woman who will likely be taking his job. She's liked by both sides, and a good choice for the position. But, first and foremost, she's a lawyer."

"What about Charity?" Deuce asked.

Travis considered Deuce's eyes for a moment. "That's the good news I was talking about. I already sent her a message to start this way. I'd like to bring her back to a job. She'll need some time to decompress and be debriefed, maybe a week, but it would be better if she already had a position waiting that she could step right into."

Deuce grinned. "I know a private security company that would jump at the chance to hire her, based only on her martial arts training. Probably several."

"I'll work on getting our girl home," Travis said. "It may take a while. She's off the grid for two weeks, after just completing a mission."

The food came out and Travis ate quickly, then joined Deuce and his wife on the dock. Having grown up here, Julie knew the water much better than her husband, so she drove the boat. Half an hour of winding and twisting through water that was only inches deep on either side of the boat, they finally reached their destination.

Several people stood grouped on the pier as Julie idled the skiff toward it. Deuce went up to the bow and readied a dock line. On the pier, a tall, tan man, his brown hair streaked by the sun, separated himself from the group. Deuce tossed him the line.

When the boat was secure, Travis stood up and fixed his gaze on the reserved man standing over him. He knew the man's background well—better than most. He also knew the background information that hadn't ever been written about, in any government document.

"How've you been, Jesse?" Travis asked.

"As well as can be expected, Colonel. What are you doing here?"

Jesse McDermitt was a no-nonsense man who played by a set of very strict but simple rules. His own rules. Trust, honor, and a strong moral compass guided him. Travis had gone afoul of that trust, though he knew that the man before him would have done the same thing in the same position.

Travis looked down at the dock, then back up at McDermitt with a questioning gaze. McDermitt nodded his consent and Travis stepped up onto the pier in front of him, each man's eyes fixed on the others.

"My time is short, too," Stockwell said. "I'm here to beg for my old job."

"Position's been filled," McDermitt said, his voice low and even. "I do have an opening for a sea-faring galley wench, if you know anyone looking for a job."

Stockwell grinned. This subject had been a thorn between them for over a year. It was McDermitt's digging and putting things together that had forced Stockwell to finally lay out to the rest of the team what had really happened to Charity.

"I just might have someone in mind," Travis said, with a wink. "She even has her own boat. Last I heard, she was on her way here. In the meantime, Deuce tells me that he needs some specialized equipment."

McDermitt nodded warily. "What kind of equipment?"

"Just about anything you want," Travis replied. "Bargain basement prices, too. Except weapons. We both know you have more than enough of those to go around."

McDermitt's eyes squinted slightly, already suspicious. "You mean like the electronics we were already planning to use?"

"We'll just call this a trial. Play with the stuff and see if it's something you'll be interested in."

"We can talk price once Devon and I get back."

"Devon?" Travis asked, and turned to look at the attractive blond woman next to McDermitt. "Detective Evans, I presume."

The woman's reaction was slightly cold and detached, much like McDermitt's reception. "And you are?" she asked in an even tone, shaking his hand.

"Travis," he replied, ignoring the icy tone. "Soon-to-be former Associate Director Stockwell with Homeland Security, and Colonel Stockwell, US Army, before that."

"We're just about to get underway, Colonel," McDermitt interrupted. "You planning to stay a while?"

"Actually, I thought I might go with you," Travis said, turning back to McDermitt with a smile. "Deuce explained what's going on, when he picked me up early this morning. Don't you think a star of Detective Evans's caliber would have two bodyguards?"

The man shrugged his broad shoulders. "This is her sting. If it's okay with her, it's fine by me."

"Can I speak to you, privately?" Evans asked, nodding her head toward the stairs. The two went up and disappeared inside McDermitt's little house.

"Is that right, Colonel?" the only black man in the group asked. "Charity's coming back?" Formerly a Navy petty officer, Tony Jacobs had been with Deuce for many years, serving under the then SEAL team commander. Jacobs had followed Deuce to DHS.

The week before, Travis had contacted Tony concerning an early retirement, and the man had accepted the conditions readily to join Deuce's new venture.

"It'll be up to her, Tony," Travis said. "But her last mission was in fact her *last* mission."

"It'll be good to see her again," Andrew Bourke said. He was a big, barrel-chested man with a deep baritone voice and thick mustache. Formerly with the same Coast Guard outfit that Deuce's wife, Julie came from, he'd been with Deuce's team for a few years now.

Another man stood silent, off to the side. He was older than most of Deuce's team. A former Chicago detective, Paul Bender had been with the Secret Service's Presidential Protection Detail until Travis recruited him over a year before. Paul held a PhD in criminal psychology and usually stayed off to one side, listening. He only spoke if asked a question, or if he had relevant information to share.

"Never met her," Paul said. "But, I've heard of her exploits, and would love to sit down and talk with her someday."

Travis nodded his understanding of the underlying statement. Paul would be the lead psychologist in debriefing Charity, then he would resign from public service to join the others.

McDermitt and Detective Evans came back down the steps. McDermitt jerked a thumb toward a door in the lower part of the house. "Put your bag in the Cigarette."

"We're not taking the big boat?" Detective Evans asked.

"Not flashy enough," McDermitt replied, as Travis lifted his go-bag out of the skiff and headed toward the door. "A Hollywood star wouldn't be riding around in a fishing boat."

"Speaking of which," another woman said from the top of the steps, as Travis disappeared through the door. He recognized the Alabama accent of Chyrel Koshinski, one of the most gifted computer analysts employed by the CIA. Deuce had recruited her over to DHS before Travis had taken over as head of the CCC. Through the open door, he could hear her talking as he dropped his bag in the long sleek boat under the house. "Your alias," she said. "You can study it on the way down. Instead of building a fake one, you're just going to impersonate someone."

"Who?" Travis heard McDermitt ask. He watched from the shadows as the detective opened the folder. She took a picture and handed it to McDermitt.

"I'm Dona Vegas," Evans said.

McDermitt studied the photo she'd handed him for a moment. "Who is she?" he asked, handing it back to the detective.

"She's a Brazilian national," Koshinski replied. "German father and Brazilian mother, born in seventy-five. She's split her time living in California and Germany for most of the last decade, though. She speaks fluent Portuguese and German, and her English has very little accent. But she can turn that up a notch on film. Some people like that."

"I don't even want to know how you know this, Chyrel," McDermitt said, with a bit of a chuckle. "So, she's a real-life porn star?"

"Yeah," Koshinski replied. "Pretty big name in the late nineties, with over a dozen films to her credit."

"What if these guys know she's Brazilian?" the detective asked.

"Leave that to us," Travis said, stepping through the doorway. "We'll come up with a diversion or change the subject. Jesse's good at improvising. All you have to do is look beautiful and be aloof."

Koshinski didn't seem the least surprised when her boss's boss suddenly appeared. She had a good poker face.

Something they probably teach in Spook School, Travis thought.

Detective Evans gave a startled look. "Yikes! I didn't even think about clothes. What's a stripper wear, when they actually wear stuff?"

Deuce's wife lifted a small bag from the boat. "Got you covered," she said. "Try some of these out while you're on the way down there. Everything should fit, just whatever you're comfortable with."

"You guys think of everything," the detective said, accepting the case.

"I spoke with Lieutenant Morgan half an hour ago," Deuce said, "when we were headed up here. He'll have two other undercover detectives inside the bar, and said you'd know who they were. He also said he tried to call you, but it went straight to voicemail. Oh, and Tony and Andrew will go with you and stay in the boat, as backup."

"How far away will they be?" Devon asked.

"Less than a hundred feet," McDermitt replied. "The rear parking lot of Rafferty's Pub is on a canal and we'll be docking there."

"You'd better get a move on," Koshinski said. "I called the club last night to arrange an interview, pretending to be your personal assistant. The owner wasn't there, but the bartender, a guy named Kenny Whitt, said he's almost always there by noon. He went ahead and made the appointment and promised to call the boss and make sure he's there. Apparently, he's at least heard the name Dona Vegas."

Just then, Detective Evans's phone rang. She fished it out of her purse, looked at the caller ID and pushed the *Accept* button, putting the phone to her ear. "Detective Evans."

Travis could just hear the tinny sound of the voice on the other end. Though he couldn't make out a word of it, the person sounded agitated about something.

"Mister Montrose, slow down," Evans said. "Who are you again?" She paused, listening. "Oh, yeah. What's this about?" She listened for a few seconds, thanked whoever it was, and ended the call.

"Surprised you got a signal down here," McDermitt said, pointing up the steps. "Usually the only place we can get one is up there on the deck."

"That was Kevin Montrose," Evans said, putting her phone away. "The gentleman who found the third body. He says he knows who the killer is and just saw him in Marathon."

"How's he know that?" McDermitt asked.

"Dunno," she replied. "Seemed like a harmless old fisherman, when I met him. I'll call the sub-station in Marathon and have them send someone to take his statement."

"He is harmless," Julie said. "I've known him all my life. He used to carry the mail, but he retired a long time ago. Now he just fishes and gossips."

McDermitt started toward the open door under the house. "We'd better get this show on the water."

While everyone boarded and stowed their personal gear, McDermitt started the powerful inboard engines. They rumbled at an idle as he pushed a button on the boat's key fob and the door in front of them began to slowly swing open. A few minutes later, the sleek racing boat idled into Harbor Channel and turned northeast.

Travis was in the port seat of the dual-console boat, familiarizing himself with the second set of gauges displayed on the dash in front of him. At the speed the boat was capable of, the driver didn't have time to monitor gauges. That would be up to Travis.

They'd done this a time or two the previous year when Travis had worked for McDermitt, so a quick glance was all he needed. His job with McDermitt had just been a cover—something McDermitt hadn't been made aware of, and another tick mark against Travis's tally in McDermitt's eyes.

But the cover had worked well, and Deuce had done a good job in DC, filling in for him in his absence.

Travis's satellite phone vibrated in his pocket and he took it out. Charity had saved a new message in their email draft folder. When he opened it, Travis expected the usual *Will do* response, or perhaps even some excitement over the fact that she was coming home. Instead, it read: *Busy now. We'll talk more on this later. CS*

CHAPTER EIGHT:

Once his yacht was securely anchored, Brad Whitaker told his captain, a leather-skinned, gray-haired man of fifty named Glen Clark, to go ashore with the crew, but check in every evening before sunset. Brad and Glen had met many years before and had become fast friends, despite the fifteen-year gap in age.

"If nothing changes," Brad said, "the crew will have three days with pay and nothing to do. But I need you back here in two."

"I'm sure they'll be genuinely broken-hearted," Glen said, with a grin. He had a company card and would pay for the hotel rooms with that. Brad Whitaker took good care of his crew, which usually numbered six or more, but this time only three.

Captain Clark's first mate, Bo Hamilton, was a younger version of Glen, and a man both Glen and Brad trusted. The ship's cook was a thirty-something woman named Virginia Crosby, who had signed on a year earlier, mostly because neither Glen nor Brad could cook. The third was a young Puerto Rican man, who crewed in exchange for passage and wouldn't be returning—a common enough occurrence in the Caribbean.

It was nearly sunset when Glen left in one of the yacht's motor launches, taking the crew and leaving his boss alone on board. Brad went to the galley and opened the door to the electric wine cellar built into the bulkhead beside the refrigerator. He took a bottle at random, gathered a glass, a small tub of ice, and a corkscrew, and went up to the aft sun deck to relax.

Pouring a glass of chardonnay, Brad placed the bottle in the tub and sat down in one of the deck chairs, facing the setting sun. The bay was nearly empty, the quickly darkening sky ablaze to the west, and it was a warm day.

"You've blocked my view," Brad heard a voice call out from behind him. He turned and looked out over the port bow, then rose, glass in hand, and went to the rail. About two hundred feet forward and a little closer to shore was an older wooden sailboat. Beyond it, a slightly larger sailboat lay at anchor.

A blond woman stood in the cockpit of the nearer boat, the line to a dinghy in her hand. Even from this distance, Brad could see the woman was strikingly beautiful. The golden glow from the sun seemed to bring out the rich texture and highlights in her shoulder-length blond hair and worked to deepen her tan. She stood facing him, hands on her narrow waist.

"My apologies," Brad shouted over the water. "But I've already sent the crew ashore. I'll have them move us tomorrow if you like. In the meantime," Brad said, raising his glass, "you're welcome to join me."

She was too far away for him to judge her reaction, but after a moment, she climbed down into the dinghy and pulled on the starter cord.

Brad had always been able to charm the women; it was a natural gift.

A moment later, she idled up to the side of Brad's yacht and turned off the engine. Though slightly disheveled, the woman was even more beautiful up close: high cheekbones, narrow nose, and a body that seemed sculpted by some long-dead artisan.

"I really do apologize," Brad said, smiling broadly. "I was busy in my office when we anchored. And, as I said, the crew has left for the evening. I'd be more than happy to share my view and a bottle of wine."

The blonde in the dinghy looked up at him and removed her sunglasses. Her exotic green eyes looked impossibly deep. She wore a loose-fitting, pale blue tank top and khaki boater's shorts. She followed the yacht's lines forward and up to the soaring bridge.

"This has to be the ugliest thing I've ever seen on the water," she said.

Brad was somewhat taken aback. "I beg your pardon."

"It has no soul," the woman said. "It's just steel and glass. You might as well watch the sunset from a condo balcony."

She pulled on the starter, the engine caught, and she put the motor into gear and roared away, leaving Brad speechless.

He turned away from the rail and started to go back to his chair. The arrangement of the small outdoor dining table and chairs on the sundeck suddenly looked just like something on a retirement condo's patio or balcony.

Looking back at the woman in the little dinghy, Brad saw that she was nearly to the beach. He took his phone from his pocket and took a picture of the woman's boat. Then he sent the picture to Clark's phone, asking if he knew what kind of boat it was.

No soul? he thought, sitting back down. *Boats don't have souls.* To his architectural brain, his yacht was perfect for his needs. Only a few years old and over a hundred feet in length, it could accommodate almost any kind of social or business function he needed it to, up to a full-blown convention. And should the need arise, he could have it moved from one place to another at over forty miles per hour, or run at half that speed for days on end.

Brad looked toward the setting sun and contemplated calling his associate on the island, just to see how the softening-up was coming along. A good sales pitch ahead of his meetings with potential sellers always helped smooth things along. He hoped to be able to move quickly on a few properties in the area.

Even if he couldn't get the properties he really needed, and the resort wasn't able go through, he could just sit on the properties he was sure he could get, and turn them for a healthy profit in a few months. And he wouldn't even have to do anything to them, aside from a quick clean-up.

But in this case everything looked promising. All but two of the properties he wanted were owned by locals, most as income-producing little villas. The two who didn't live on the island had already hinted at their readiness to sell. More often than not, it was the remote owners who were most difficult to negotiate with.

Looking back over his shoulder again, Brad could see the woman's dinghy on the beach, along with another slightly larger one. But he didn't see anyone on the small beach. His eyes caught movement and he looked higher. There was a house on the bluff, only the upper third of which was visible. A pale blue glow danced across the walls as the swimming pool lights began to envelop the house, slowly overwhelming the growing darkness.

A man and a woman were silhouetted against the reflected pool lights. They were leaning against a rail that appeared to surround the deck. After a moment, they turned and went back toward the house.

Brad's phone vibrated in his hand and he looked at it. It was a reply from Glen. *Not sure who built it, but it's a classic John Alden design, and quite a beauty. Probably sixty to eighty years old, I'd guess. I was admiring her when we anchored. You're suddenly interested in boats?*

Brad chuckled. Boats—like planes, cars, and hammers—were tools. Whether you used one as transportation, a status symbol, or as a tool to close a business deal or to charm some wide-eyed young woman out of her clothes, it made no difference.

Brad Whitaker had grown up using tools, and he was good with them. He knew which ones to use, and he knew when and where to use them to accomplish the task at hand. This job called for a display of success, wealth, and power. The people he'd be meeting were well-to-do, old money from colonial days. They respected the kind of financial muscle Brad could flex.

Then he'd use another tool to try to convince the land-owners to deal with him. That tool was his natural charm. It had been said, during his college years, that he could charm the rattle from snake or baby.

Brad glanced at the house once more. The blue pool lights were off, and a soft white glow emanated from the back windows of the house. He was pretty sure it was one of the properties he was planning to make an offer on.

Again, the phone in Brad's hand vibrated and he looked at the display. Pushing the *Accept* button, he put the phone to his ear. "Hope you're calling with good news."

The tone of the man's voice on the other end told him immediately that negotiations hadn't gone as expected.

He listened for a moment, astounded by the turn of events. Finally, he said, "Yes, I agree. It seems I have no choice but to pay the higher price. Contact the property owners one more time tonight. If things go well on your end, I can make an offer tomorrow."

After a moment, Brad said, "Yes, I'm in Magens Bay. Just arrived a couple of hours ago. We'll be ready for your delivery in two days, no problem."

Ending the call, Brad put the phone in his pocket. It was now fully dark. With the moon below the horizon, the sky was ablaze with stars. As he sipped his wine, he considered what he'd just learned.

Several of the local owners of the properties he was interested in had reacted favorably to the first discreet contact, which had been over a month before. Two had been adamant that they weren't interested in selling, and a handful of others were on the fence.

The fence sitters weren't a concern, but the two who flatly said no would need to be the focus of negotiations; one of them owned three of the properties he was interested in buying.

Money was another tool that Brad used very successfully. He knew that if he threw enough money at a problem, it usually went away. Adding a little more financial incentive in the early stages of negotiations could mean a thousand-fold increase at the end of the project. And his associate here on Saint Thomas would know exactly what to do with that money.

Glancing up at the house on the ridge, Brad thought of the woman from the sailboat. She intrigued him. He somehow knew that the boat she'd been standing on was her own and didn't belong to the man in the house. Was he the owner of the house and she a wayfaring sailor with a man in every port?

Brad had met his share of beautiful women, but the drifters and loners who lived on boats, though a tough and capable breed, tended to be a bit weathered. Any women among this crowd were far outnumbered. Even more rare were the solo women cruisers. Add to that this woman's natural beauty, and it was like finding a diamond among the billions of billions grains of sand on a beach.

He looked again at the picture he'd taken of her boat. The lines were clean, simple, and functional-looking. In a day and time nearly a hundred years ago, one might even have said *elegant*.

The night sounds enveloped Brad. The soft lapping of tiny waves against the long steel hull, the muted creak of the woman's wooden boat, along with the sporadic clinking sound of a halyard against aluminum, combined with the night cries of birds and the occasional whoosh of a dolphin exhaling on the surface.

Tomorrow would be all about business, but tonight he just wanted to unwind and ignore the outside world for a few hours. Brad Whitaker was fine with isolation. He didn't need the noise of the city. Leave the TV, blaring music, car horns, and conversation to those who liked living in boxes.

Eventually, Brad slipped into a light sleep, his chin resting on his chest.

His nap was short lived. He bolted upright, the sound of firecrackers coming from far ahead of the yacht's bow. He moved quickly to the starboard rail. Somewhere above Magens Beach, half a mile away, he could hear popping sounds, as if someone were celebrating something.

When he heard several quick, mechanical bursts of pops, he realized it wasn't fireworks, but gunfire.

"What in the hell is going on up there?"

CHAPTER NINE

Things developed quickly, and for several hours Travis didn't have a chance to reply to the cryptic message from Charity. Not that it mattered. She was on stand-down in the Virgin Islands, and they'd agreed that during that time there would be no more than one contact a day, unless it were an emergency.

With daylight fading, Travis stood on a fishing pier with Andrew Bourke and Tony Jacobs, watching as the EMTs slammed the door on the back of the ambulance. The man inside, shot twice, had been on a steroid-induced rant, but was now whining like a little girl, handcuffed to the stretcher and apparently paralyzed below the waist.

As the ambulance took off, lights flashing and siren wailing, Travis turned and watched several more emergency personnel on the beach. They lifted a stretcher from the stern of an old fishing boat. The Cigarette boat that had brought them to Bahia Honda from Key West, lay next to the old man's fishing boat, holed by the rocks, with a possible blown engine. The old man was on the stretcher, a white sheet covering his head.

McDermitt followed the procession of men up the rocky path to the parking lot where another ambulance waited. The lights on this ambulance were off. Travis and the two men went down to the parking lot to join the others.

"You all right?" Bourke asked McDermitt, who stood watching the medical people lift the body into the ambulance.

McDermitt was covered in blood. "Yeah, Andrew," he sighed, looking down at his clothes. "It's not my blood."

"Who was he?" Travis asked. "Anyone you know?"

"I've seen him around some," McDermitt replied as the ambulance pulled away. "Never met him, though. He was one of yours."

"One of mine?"

"Eighty-Second," McDermitt said, taking a couple of steps after the ambulance, then stopping. "Jumped into Sicily and Anzio." He turned and faced Travis as a brown Ford sedan pulled into the parking lot, its headlights washing over the group of men. "Why didn't you put a bullet in his head and be done with it?"

"Too many witnesses," Travis replied, tapping out a message on his phone. "He's going away for a long time, and I have a feeling he's not going to like what happens."

"Who you contacting, Colonel?" Tony asked.

"Friends at Bragg."

The brown Ford stopped. Detective Evans and her partner, Lieutenant Ben Morgan, got out and walked toward them. Morgan was a middle-aged man, balding and a little overweight. Travis had only met him one other time—under similar circumstances, except it was pouring rain then.

"I hope that's not your blood," Morgan said.

"It's not," McDermitt replied. "We got here just a few seconds too late, Lieutenant. Montrose is dead."

It took several hours for the detectives and forensics people to process the pier and the boat. McDermitt spent the time arranging to get his wrecked go-fast boat removed from the beach, and the others helped the detectives any way they could.

With the others busy, Travis sat down on a rock and reread the message from Charity. *What the hell did she mean, we'll talk about it later?* he thought. He knew she could be a little unbalanced at times, but it was something she had full control over. Besides, there were occasions when unbalanced was what you needed.

"What's up, Colonel?" McDermitt said, sitting quietly on a rock next to him.

Travis hadn't even heard him approach; for a man his size, he was surprisingly light on his feet.

"Eighty-Second, you said?" Travis replied, changing to a different app on his phone and tapping some keys.

"Yeah. Toward the end of the war, the invasion of Italy."

"Found him," Travis said, turning the screen to McDermitt, showing him a picture of Kevin Montrose, many years younger and in uniform. "Silver star for actions at Anzio. Mind if I take the lead on contacting his next of kin and making arrangements?"

"Sure," McDermitt replied, as Tony and Andrew joined them.

"Anyone call about a ride?" Tony said. "If we have to wait for the police to finish, it could be a while."

"I called Deuce," Jesse said. "He'll be here in a few minutes."

When Deuce arrived in his wife's yellow Cherokee, he spoke with Lieutenant Morgan for a moment before walking over to the four men.

"Director," Deuce said, nodding. "Morgan said that, in deference to your current standing with the government, he'll catch up with the four of you tomorrow."

"Then let's get out of here," McDermitt said, rising, and walking toward the Cherokee.

The ride back to Marathon didn't take long and there was little talk along the way. When they turned off the highway onto the shell driveway to the *Rusty Anchor*, Travis pulled up the message from Charity and handed his phone to Deuce.

"What do you make of this?" he asked, as Deuce parked the car. "It's Charity's reply, after I ordered her to return to Homestead."

Deuce read the message. "'We'll talk about this later?'" Deuce said. "What's to talk about?"

"What exactly was your message to her?" McDermitt asked from the back seat.

"No way to pull it up," Travis said. "'Stand down, return to Homestead. It's over.' Or words to that effect."

McDermitt leaned forward in the seat. "I told you before, Colonel. She's damaged goods, not completely right in the head. What the hell have you been having her do?"

Travis shifted in his seat and looked back at Jesse. "It no longer matters. She has orders to return home."

"It matters to us," Bourke said. "Jesse's right. All that shit she went through in Afghanistan, then losing that Williams kid? We're more than just former co-workers, Colonel. We have a right to know."

Travis appraised the big man sitting behind him. "That's national security, Andrew. Not something—"

Deuce slammed a fist on the wheel of the car. "That's bullshit, Colonel!"

The outburst was completely unexpected and totally out of character. Deuce was always the calm, cool head in any situation.

Turning in his seat, he eyed Travis. "You want me to hire her, but you won't tell me her background? That message was *not* the response it should have been."

All five were silent for a moment. Finally, Travis looked around at the four men with him. "This doesn't leave this car," he said. "Only her first mission was against terrorists. She screwed up, and there was a lot of unanticipated collateral damage."

"Doesn't sound like her at all," McDermitt interrupted. "Civilians?"

"No," Travis said. "Her target was one man, the leader of a terrorist cell training in Mexico. She killed him first, then one by one, killed all of them. Some were burned alive."

"I don't see any problem in that," Jesse said, offhanded. "Not one bit."

"One was a deep-cover CIA operative, Jesse."

"Does the agency know?" Tony asked.

"No," Travis replied. "You watched most of it, Tony. Then Deuce had you destroy the evidence."

"I knew that was her," Tony said. "One of those guys was a good guy?"

"Yeah, but only the four of us—and perhaps Miss Koshinski—know how he died. The Agency called the mission a failure. I raised holy hell with them for not letting us know they had a man on the inside. Since then, the Agency has been keeping her busy with other missions that have nothing to do with national security—at least not directly. She's gone after land barons, cartel kingpins, even smuggled a couple out of Cuba. None of which had a direct impact on the so-called War on Terror. But all were sanctioned by the SecDef and, by default, POTUS himself."

"And now," McDermitt grumbled, "you have a psychologically imbalanced woman out there, a person who we all helped to make, ignoring your orders to stand down. What kind of dirty laundry is she cleaning up this week for the CIA?"

"That's just it," Travis said. "She's not on a mission. She's supposed to be resting and relaxing in the Virgin Islands after the Cuba thing."

"I don't get it," Andrew said. "If she's not on a mission, what's there to talk about?"

"Have you messaged her and asked her to elaborate?" Deuce asked.

"Wouldn't matter," Travis replied. "We don't communicate more than once per day."

Deuce glanced at his watch. "Well, it'll be tomorrow in just a few minutes. In the VI, it's already tomorrow. You should call her."

"Phone calls don't work," Travis said. "She keeps her satellite phone turned off, but checks for messages several times a day. Odds are any message I send now won't be read until morning."

Deuce handed the phone back. "Order her to go to the Content Keys."

"To Jesse's house?"

"Yeah," Deuce replied, opening his door. "She trusts him. And, for some reason, she doesn't appear to trust you."

CHAPTER TEN:

After dinner, Charity and Victor watched the sun go down across the bay. The pool lights switched on automatically, a soft blue glow spreading across the deck in the gathering dusk.

"He actually hit on you?" Victor asked.

"I wouldn't go that far," Charity replied, as they turned and walked back toward the house. "He just said his crew was gone, and offered to share his view and his wine on his gazillion dollar mega-yacht, which I told him was ugly."

Entering the house, Victor laughed and switched off the pool lights. "Just like that? You called his boat ugly?"

"I told him that I thought his boat was the ugliest thing I'd ever seen on the water. I mean, come on, it's all steel and glass."

They went into his room, and once more climbed up to the rooftop. Earlier, they'd had to rebuild the blind, when a gust of wind had pulled one side loose. Victor had found a hammer and some nails and had secured two sides to the rails. They'd dragged another lounge chair over to hold the loose end up better, creating a sort of kid-style tent.

"Well, it is a butt-ugly boat," Victor said, taking a seat. "So you're going to return home?"

"I never said I was," Charity replied. "I just don't know. If you're right, and it's just a movement of people before the new administration takes office, wouldn't he have said that?"

"I don't know the guy. What's he like?"

"Well, there *is* that," Charity replied. "He's a man of few words. And a former Army Colonel."

Victor thought about it for a moment, stretching his tanned legs out on the lounge chair. "Do you trust him?"

It was Charity's turn to think. "For the most part, yeah," she finally replied. "But he's lied about things in the past, and he's good at it. So, no, I don't trust him completely."

"Anyone else in your old organization who you trust?"

"My boss, Deuce Livingston. And you know McDermitt. I trust both of them completely."

"Any way you can contact one of them? See what's going on?"

"No. Not any way that couldn't be intercepted if someone was monitoring them."

They watched the stars for a while and talked about ordinary subjects. Victor even made Charity laugh, something she hadn't done a lot of in the last year and a half.

Charity's laptop made a beeping sound. They'd brought it up to monitor the motion sensors on the hill above Magens Beach.

Quickly the two of them went to the nest and crawled beneath the tarp. Charity glanced at the computer screen.

"It's number four," she said. "The one you put highest on the hillside."

Victor already had the spotting scope up and was looking through it. Charity pulled the stock of her rifle in close to her shoulder, adjusting it against her cheek, as she too looked at the road through the gray-green night optics.

"Two cars parked just this side of the pass, facing away," Victor said. "More than half a dozen men standing on the road, near where we put the sensors. Range to the men on the hill is eleven-hundred and four yards, inclination is plus four degrees."

"Got 'em," Charity said, seeing the group on the hill and calculating the trajectory in her head. All but one wore the dreadlocks popular in Jamaica and some other islands. The one with the shorter hairstyle seemed to be in charge, pointing and talking. All were armed with rifles.

Looking down the slope slightly, she saw one man standing away from the group, urinating beside a bush.

"They're starting down the hill," Victor whispered.

Charity wasted no time. These men were heavily armed and seemed bent on getting to the village. She chambered a round, aimed, and fired. The rifle recoiled against her shoulder, the shot making no more noise than a hand-clap.

Victor chuckled. "I think he got himself stuck trying to zip up."

Chambering another round, Charity moved the night vision scope down the hill, quickly finding the other men. They seemed to be looking back up the hill to the first man. She spotted a large volcanic rock between three men, one of them being the leader of the group. She fired quickly, then ratcheted the bolt. The brass cartridge skittered across the deck.

Muzzle flashes appeared on the hillside, followed by the distinctive sound of gunfire a moment later.

"What the hell are they shooting at?" Victor asked.

Charity watched through the scope as the men on the hillside fired blindly down the hill. "They're panicked," she said, bringing the crosshairs to bear on the leader. She knew she could end this immediately with a single shot. The others would scatter like so many cockroaches when the light comes on.

Her finger tightened on the trigger, taking up the slack. It would be so easy. Her cheek moved imperceptibly, just before the rifle recoiled once more.

"Ha!" Victor said. "That one did it. They're pulling back."

The last bullet struck a large, dead, tree branch just above the leader's head. It broke off and hit the man squarely on top of the head.

"Their gunfire is bound to draw the cops," Victor said.

"Let's make sure," Charity whispered, moving the reticles to the two vehicles parked on the hilltop. "Range to the cars?"

Victor moved his scope. "Range is thirteen-hundred and thirty-nine yards, Charity," he said, slightly dismayed. "Inclination is four point five degrees."

The men had turned the cars around before descending the hill—probably in case they had to make a hasty retreat, which they were now doing. She recognized the small thirty-some-year-old hatchback with the fake wood paneling that was parked closest.

With the running men still a good hundred yards from their cars, the rifle recoiled once more against Charity's shoulder. The Ford Pinto blossomed into a bright fireball, negating the scope's ability to adjust to the intense light.

Charity raised her eye from the scope and looked out across the bay. An orange and black cloud billowed from the road just below the pass. Rolling violently upward, the fireball ignited the brush and palms around the destroyed car.

"Guess they didn't get the recall notice on those things," Victor said.

Charity switched to day optics and counted seven men, backlit against the flames, as they shielded themselves from it and ran to the other car. It wasn't a big car, but they all somehow got inside and disappeared over the pass. A moment later, sirens could be heard, far in the distance.

Victor lowered the spotting scope. The smell of spent gunpowder hung heavy in the confined space. "If I hadn't seen it, I never would have believed it. That was an uphill shot from three-quarters of a mile."

"The gas tanks on those things are a big target," Charity said.

"Think they know you've been missing intentionally?"

Charity began to scoot backward to get to fresh air. "The tree branch might have been a giveaway."

Victor joined her at the deck rail and looked toward the pass. The car was burning furiously.

"About contacting one of those two you trust," he said, picking up the earlier conversation as if nothing had happened. "McDermitt's a charter guy, right?"

"Yeah, at first I thought it was just his cover job and he was an integral part of the team. But later I learned he really does run a charter business and was just doing freelance work for Deuce, my old boss."

"Think he has a website? A way to book a charter online?"

Charity glanced at her laptop. Victor had already scanned it for a listening device before bringing it up. "Of course," she said, going toward it. "Why didn't I think of that?"

Victor put a hand on her arm. "Wait. Your computer still might not be secure, and I bet your phone isn't either."

"You have a laptop," Charity said. "You read books on it."

Victor looked shocked. "Yeah, well sometimes I do. I actually prefer a real book, though. I use the laptop for writing. We can use it, if I can get a wifi signal."

"You write?"

"Sort of working on a novel," he replied, sheepishly.

"That's commendable," she said with a smile. "There's an Ethernet outlet in the living room. Do you have a cable?"

Just below, a doorbell rang and they both immediately drew their sidearms. "Who the hell could that be?" Victor said.

The bell rang again, then twice more. "Better go see," Charity said. "Those guys won't be back for a while, if at all."

Together, they went quickly down the ladder and toward the front of the house. They approached the door cautiously, and Victor peered through a slit in the curtains next to the door.

"It's Henri," he said, turning on the porch light and shoving the big Kimber into the back of his pants.

Charity holstered her own weapon as Victor swung the door open.

"Rene, thank God you are safe," Henri said, a heavy sigh in his voice. "There has been some shooting on the road above the beach. And an explosion."

Lisette hurried past him to Charity. "We saw the two of you walking up the road earlier and were worried you might have done something and been hurt."

"We're fine," Charity said. "Nobody has been hurt."

Victor stepped aside and waved Henri inside. He was followed by Chet and two other islanders Victor recognized but had never met. Behind them was a tall white man dressed in casual but expensive-looking clothes.

Charity's face flushed just a little when she saw him.

Henri introduced the two islanders as Phil Majors and William Harington. "They own property here on the peninsula, too," Henri said. "And this gentleman, we just met in front of the villa."

"My apologies," the stranger said. "I'm on the yacht anchored off the beach here. I heard the commotion and decided I should see what was going on. My name's Brad Whitaker."

"We've met," Charity said, eyeing the man cautiously. "Please, come in. Does anyone know what the shooting was about?"

Victor closed and locked the door, then led everyone into the living room.

"The police are on the way," Henri said. "This is terrible. First Chet's bar, and now this. We have no idea who was shooting or why."

"We've had offers on our properties," Phil Majors blurted out. He was a smallish, dark-skinned man, with obsidian dark eyes.

"I wasn't planning to sell," William chimed in, "but if things keep going like this, I'll have no choice."

William was the opposite of Phil in just about every way that Charity could see. Tall and a little overweight, he had a light complexion and light brown eyes. It was obvious that he and Phil were a couple.

"If the buyer finds out," Phil said, turning to his partner, "he'll lower the offer."

"I'm afraid he already knows," Whitaker said.

All eyes in the room turned toward the stranger.

"It's you?" William said, his hand going to his throat.

"Yes," Whitaker replied. "I'm a real estate developer. But please. My offer is still good."

"But the shooting," Phil said. "The explosion."

"Mister Majors, I'm from LA," Whitaker said, as if that dismissed everything. "I'm sure the police will have a handle on any kind of illegal activity."

"Do you always come ashore late at night to discuss business, Mister Whitaker?" Charity asked.

Whitaker smiled, his teeth white and perfect. "Some of the best deals are made after the sun goes down. But no. I came ashore several hours ago and sought these folks out when I heard the gunfire."

"At any rate," Henri said, extending a rolled-up towel to Victor, "I thought you might want this."

Victor took it, noticing its weight, and carefully unrolled it. He looked up at his old friend. "Really, Henri?"

"I have another," the islander replied with a shrug. "Just in case these men mean trouble, as you suggested."

Victor pushed the gun back to him. "This is a piece of art," he said. "And you forget, you've told me of its history. This should be in a museum."

"Besides," Charity said, turning her back slightly, and raising her shirt to expose her Sig, "we're armed well enough."

"Is there something I'm missing?" Whitaker asked. "This should be a matter for the police."

Victor turned toward Whitaker. "The police are on the other side of the island, Mister Whitaker. If anything happens over here, the response time is about a quarter of an hour."

"I see," the man said. "You and the other locals have to take care of yourselves in the event of trouble."

Charity listened to his words carefully. His voice was a deep baritone, very smooth and articulate. At home in the boardroom or the bedroom. The kind of voice people listened to. In her mind, the rich playboy seemed disingenuous somehow. He seemed to be fishing for something.

He was as tall as Victor and they had similar builds, but that was where the similarities ended. Victor's hands were calloused, forearms corded with muscle from hauling sheets and halyards.

Whitaker's hand had been soft when she shook it, and though he was muscular, she could tell it was gym muscle. Probably three times a week, at least.

"I don't live here," Victor said to Whitaker, extending the antique revolver to Henri once more, "but these folks are my friends."

Henri took back the pistol, wrapping it gingerly in the towel. "If you are sure you don't need it."

"Thanks, no," Victor said, then pointed toward the computer outlet in the wall. "I do have a question, though. Does that work? Gabby has to take care of some business arrangements and needs internet access."

"Yes," Lisette said. "It is only a telephone connection, so it will be a little slow. But it is a dedicated line."

"I have satellite service on the yacht if you need it," Whitaker said, flashing Charity another million-watt smile.

"Thanks," she replied. "This will be fine."

"We should leave," Lisette told her husband. "These young people don't want us old folks around."

"Yes," Henri agreed. "We are sorry to be a bother."

"No bother," Victor said. "But really, we'll be just fine."

The five of them left then, but not before Whitaker's lingering handshake with Charity.

"Can you believe that guy?" Charity said after they left.

"I'm sure you get that a lot," Victor said, walking through the living room toward his room and the ladder in the closet.

"Not all that often, and definitely not when it's obvious I'm with someone else."

"You're getting sloppy."

Victor started up the ladder, leaving Charity puzzled. She'd thought she acted totally indifferent toward the man.

"What's that supposed to mean?" she asked as she climbed up after him.

"Letting strangers know we're armed," he replied.

Joining him on the roof, Charity looked out toward the big yacht. "I thought he was acting a little strangely."

"Well, he was definitely hitting on you hard enough to leave dents."

"Do I detect a little jealousy?" she asked, glad for the chance to change the subject. Victor was right, that had been a ridiculously stupid thing to do.

Victor eyed her sharply. "Just an observation. Are we sleeping up here again tonight?"

Charity started toward the cover. "It's probably a good idea."

Together, they crawled beneath the tarp again. "Seems a shame," he said, "to have this whole house, with the pool and hot tub and everything, then sleep up here on the roof."

"I like sleeping under the stars," she said. "Besides, this will come to a head, sooner rather than later. We'll enjoy it all then."

Taking up the spotting scope, Victor trained it on the distant hill. There was no need to use night vision; the lights from two police cars and a fire truck provided enough light. The fire was out. Spotlights from the various vehicles all shined on the smoking hulk.

"It'll probably be several hours before they get that car removed," Victor said. "And the cops won't leave until it's gone. Those guys aren't coming back for a while. We should get some sleep."

Down on the beach, they heard an outboard engine start and a moment later, a small boat could be heard pulling away from the shoreline.

"That must be the smarmy yacht owner," Charity said, stretching out on her sleeping bag.

Victor swung the spotting scope toward the boats at anchor below them. "Yeah, he's headed back to his boat. What time is it?"

"Just after one, local time. Why?"

"Just curious," he replied. "For someone eager to buy, he seems to be in a hurry to leave three prospective sellers, who are already up and wide awake at this hour."

Charity turned her laptop around and swiped the mouse pad with her finger to wake it up. "I should check for messages," she said, opening the mail server. "What was with Henri's pistol?"

"It's a Colt Navy revolver," Victor replied, still watching the man on the yacht. "It was once owned by Ulises Hilarión Heureaux Leibert, the former president of the Dominican Republic. He was Henri's second great-grand-uncle."

The draft folder had a new message. Charity opened and read it.

"Anything?" Victor asked.

"From my handler. He says to go to the Content Keys when I can."

"Where's that?"

She closed the laptop. "In the Middle Florida Keys," she replied. "Where Jesse lives."

"That's good, right? You said you trusted him completely."

Charity considered it a moment. "The thing is," she began, "since you put that bug in my head, I can't shake it. No matter how remote, there is a possibility that my handler said to go there because he knows I trust McDermitt. There's only one place to anchor anywhere near his house. It's way out in the back country at the end of a long natural channel."

"And you're worried it might be a trap? Hey, look, paranoia has kept me alive. Being paranoid doesn't mean that someone's *not* after you."

"So we do what we'd planned," Charity said. "Contact Jesse through his website."

"Won't that be monitored, too?" he asked, stretching out beside her.

"Don't get too comfortable. You have to go get your laptop for me."

"Tonight?" he asked, switching the scope off and setting it aside.

"Yeah, tonight," Charity replied. "I think I have a way to make it inconspicuous if his site's being monitored, which I'm sure is the case."

Victor groaned as he sat up and started for the ladder. "Be right back."

"Hurry," she said in a sultry voice.

After Victor left, she powered up the spotting scope and turned it toward Whitaker's big yacht. Light poured from nearly every window on every deck.

Such a waste of money, she thought. On *Wind Dancer*, she had to conserve everything, especially water, fuel, and electricity. But she always had. Resources should never be squandered. This man's lavish yacht was wasteful beyond measure.

She looked toward the stern and didn't see anyone. Slowly, she panned the flybridge and upper deck, all awash with interior lighting, but didn't see anyone there, either. Dropping down, she scanned the lower deck and saw Whitaker sitting alone in a huge stateroom below the pilothouse. The windows were massive and afforded anyone a view of the interior.

He was shirtless, sitting cross-legged on a large sofa, talking to someone on the phone. Charity noted his broad shoulders and thick chest. He suddenly rose from the couch, obviously upset at whomever he was talking to.

It was also obvious that he was half-naked, wearing only a pair of blue briefs. Charity felt voyeuristic and a bit uncomfortable, but she couldn't look away. He was beyond fit. Though he wasn't huge, muscle rippled through his chest and abs as he spoke on the phone.

He seemed highly agitated, every muscle in his body tensed as if he might crush the phone in his hand.

Charity watched as Whitaker stabbed a finger on the phone's screen and tossed it on a large coffee table. Then he turned and walked to the window, and seemed to be staring straight up at her. This didn't alarm her. She'd learned from one of the best. Her vantage point would be hard to spot, even with night vision. With the lights on in his stateroom, Whitaker most likely couldn't see anything at all through the glass.

Probably admiring his own reflection, she thought. He was an exceptionally handsome man, but he obviously also knew it. He probably wielded his looks the same way he did his money and power—as if a woman should just give in to his whims and feel somehow blessed that he even looked at her.

Charity put the scope down and rolled onto her back. The moon had risen and washed out most of the stars to the east, but across the bay the sky was ablaze, right down to the mountains. She stared up at the stars as if looking for guidance. Of course, she knew there wouldn't be any kind of sign from them, but they did seem to be patiently listening to her thoughts.

If there was any chance that someone would be laying a trap when she returned, they couldn't have picked a better place. McDermitt's island was surrounded by shallow water, the only approach in a boat like *Wind Dancer*, was a three-mile straight line from the northeast in a deep, natural channel, known as Harbor Channel. There was little maneuvering room in a forty-five-foot antique sailboat—but maybe she didn't have to go there aboard *Dancer*, nor go straight to his island. She knew enough about the man's habits that she should be able to come up with something different.

If her job was over, what then? Was she expendable? Or would they just give her a pink slip and wish her a happy life? If that were the case, she could just disappear now.

That thought did have a certain appeal. She had plenty of money set aside, both on hand and in numbered accounts in the Caymans. Being an assassin had some financial benefits, and the only remorse she felt for money she'd taken was that it had been taken from others before her.

Leave *Wind Dancer* and go off with Victor? She hated the idea of leaving *Dancer*, but the two of them could turn her upside down and never be certain that they'd looked everywhere for a tracking device. The government had rebuilt *Dancer* from the frames out. There could be tracking devices built right into the timbers, waiting for a signal to activate.

She'd hate to give up her boat; it had become a part of who she was. She fully understood Victor's desire to live life completely off the grid.

No, Charity thought, thinking of her friends on the team, *I'll go back. For now. I must at least try to explain to them why I did it. But I'll go back in a way and time of my choosing, a way that nobody would think of.*

She heard Victor's dinghy racing back to the beach, and a few minutes later he climbed up to the roof. "It's all set up, with a browser open," he said. "The phone line is slow and my laptop isn't the best in the world."

Charity stood and hugged Victor tightly. "I'm going back—but not how anyone will think."

Victor's expression showed his disappointment.

"I don't think it will be permanent, though," she said. "Will you go with me?"

"To the States?" He sounded alarmed.

"Not really the States," she said, walking toward the ladder. "The Conch Republic. It'll be safe. I have a plan. Or I will, if Jesse understands the message."

"I'll think about it," he said, pointing toward the lights on the far hill. "For now, I'm gonna keep an eye on what's going on up there."

Charity went down to the living room. Victor's computer was open on the small bamboo coffee table, booted up and ready. It took only a few minutes for her to set up a Yahoo email account, then she found Jesse's website and navigated to the charter booking page. The connection was very slow and the page seemed to take forever to load.

Finally, it did, and she chose a Saturday in mid-October, entered the information in the little boxes, and clicked the *Send* button.

CHAPTER ELEVEN:

Twice in as many nights, Claude Whyte had been driven away. The fact that he never even saw the man or men who so easily repelled them angered him to the core. So he was in an extra surly mood when the car finally pulled into the driveway.

The house he was renting near Estate Canaan was large, but it wasn't as big as others in the area. It had six bedrooms, which were enough for everyone in his posse.

Getting out of the passenger side as four of his men spilled out of the overcrowded backseat, Claude came around the hood of the car to Tarone McFarlane. "I ha' to make a call, mon. Pick two good men and be ready to leave in 'bout an hour wit di van."

After the others went inside, Claude scrolled through his contacts list, found the name, and tapped the *Call* button. The man answered after the first ring.

"Yuh tryin' ta get me killed?" Claude snarled into the phone. "Blood-clot, mon! Dere must be ten men down dere wit guns and dey knew we was comin'. I'm movin' up di delivery, comin' t'night. Den I gwon hit dem hard in di morning, before it gets light."

He listened for a moment. The man was obviously irate about the schedule change.

"Look, mon," Claude interrupted. "I and I don't care 'bout dat! Ya hear me? We gwon do what we said and you gwon do what you said. After dat, I think it be time to part ways."

Claude had to hold the phone away from his ear, the man was shouting so loudly. Then the phone went dead as Tarone came back outside.

"I got two men gettin' ready," he said, as he approached Claude. "They eating now. You should eat, too. Where we goin'?"

"Down to di warehouse," Claude said. "We're movin' up di delivery time, and it don't matter if dat fool is ready or not. Den, we gwon go back and find di ones shooting at us. I and I gwon cut dem up bad, mon."

An hour later, driving a nondescript white minivan, Tarone turned off the street into a fenced driveway that ended at a roll-up warehouse door.

Claude turned to the two men in the backseat and handed one of them a key. "Open up di door, mon."

The man got out, unlocked the padlock, and raised the door. Tarone put the van in gear and drove inside. The warehouse lights came on automatically as the van's headlights swept the interior of the building. The door came back down, and the rest of the men got out.

Claude went to a small interior office, unlocked the door, and flung it open. He turned on the light and, motioning the two men inside, pulled a tarp off a stack of wooden crates.

"Take di four boxes on di right," he said, stepping back out into the warehouse and lighting a spliff.

It took both men to lift each of the four heavy crates and carry them to the back of the van while Tarone and Claude shared the joint. When they were finished loading, they all got back in the van for the short drive to the dock where their boat was kept.

Tarone backed in as close to the boat as he could. It wasn't the go-fast boat they'd used on Cat Island, but a mid-sized sport-fishing boat that could run upwards of thirty knots and carry more cargo.

Jumping aboard, Tarone went to the small flybridge and started the big diesel engine. Once the men had the boxes loaded on the boat, they cast off the lines and Tarone idled out into Krum Bay, on the south side of the island.

"Where to?" Tarone asked.

"Go out into di ocean, den go west," Claude said. "We gwon meet a boat not far from here."

It took only thirty minutes to get to where the delivery boat lay at anchor, a large center console tied up to the stern platform. Tarone maneuvered the fishing boat alongside the deliveryman's boat. Two men stood on the aft deck, waiting to catch lines tossed to them; soon the big fishing boat was snug alongside.

The older of the two men opened a transom door, stepped down, and pointed toward a raised stern section with two Jet Skis inside. "Bring the boxes in here," he said, leading the way.

Tarone helped his two men get the unwieldy boxes over onto the other boat, then into the lower deck. Claude went up to the aft deck with the younger man.

"My posse go in to do a little roughin' around and end up in hospital," Claude said, his tone menacing. "Den we go back wit guns and get shot at before we halfway dere. Not what we agreed on, mon."

"I think outsiders are involved," the man said, handing Claude a thick envelope. "I've noticed two strangers in the area, a man and a woman. Both Americans."

"Dat was more dan one mon," Claude said, opening the envelope, and thumbing the wad of bills tucked inside.

"If it's the man I think, he's in the pool house on the cliff. Do whatever you want with him, but I don't want any of the locals harmed. Use the stranger as an example for them—but not tonight. Wait until tomorrow at noon." The man paused and took a step closer to the Jamaican. "Two things, Claude," he said, his eyes flashing with anger. "Be careful how you speak to me. You and I are in business together until I say we're not. Are we clear on that? Because if we're not, I can make a phone call and have someone pay a visit to your family's house in ten minutes to explain the situation to your wife. Maybe she can convince you to be civil."

Folding the envelope into his back pocket, Claude looked back at the man with the same fierce intensity. He knew this man had the means to carry out his threat, but he couldn't be seen as backing down.

"I and I will do what you say, mon," Claude said, then patted his back pocket. "And dis will just cover it. You said dere was two things."

"Don't hurt the woman. Bring her to me."

CHAPTER TWELVE:

After all the excitement at the old Bahia Honda bridge, McDermitt didn't sleep well. He'd done all he could. At least that's what he tried to convince himself of. They'd just come up a little bit short on time at the end. He felt sorry for the loss of the old man, and that he'd never gotten to know him.

Rising from the bunk in the back of his little stilt-house, he went into the front room and poured a thermos of coffee before going down to the dock area below the house. He had a laptop on his primary charter boat, *Gaspar's Revenge*. It was connected to a satellite server through an antenna mounted on the roof of the house.

He powered the machine up and did a few Google searches for Kevin Montrose, curious about the man. He read the story in the online version of the local Keys paper and saw no mention of the man's military service.

Typical of that generation, he thought. McDermitt's grandfather had fought in the South Pacific, and had rarely spoken of it.

Just before turning the machine off, he checked his email. He didn't get messages very often, and most were junk—or what his daughter called spam. There was one message from his business website: someone wanting to book a charter.

At first, he was startled when he read the name of the person on the booking request. It was an old girlfriend, someone he thought he'd never see again. It had been over two years since she'd left. What she'd written in the comments section left him scratching the stubble on the side of his face. She said she wanted to photograph individual butterfly fish, and was referred by a common friend.

Being an avid diver, as well as taking out occasional dive charters, McDermitt knew a little about butterfly fish. They were rarely seen singly, but most often in mated pairs, something most underwater photographers would know.

Suddenly, all three things hit his mind at once and triggered a memory. It was several months after the death of his wife. McDermitt had met Tina LaMons in Key West and they'd spent several days together. She'd been a bartender and reserve deputy.

As things turned out, Tina knew Charity, who'd only recently joined Deuce's team. They'd both been vying for a spot on the Olympic swim team six years before that. Tina hadn't made the finals due to an injury, and Charity had won a bronze medal in the individual medley. Part of which was the butterfly stroke.

The mutual friend that was mentioned in the comments was just the first name, Jared. McDermitt knew of only one Jared. He'd been a bouncer where Tina used to work. She'd left to return to the family farm in the Midwest several months before he'd been killed by an IED right behind the *Rusty Anchor*. In the days leading up to his death, Jared and Charity had met and seemed to have formed a bond. She'd been heartbroken when he was killed. The man who'd sent the bomb was Stockwell's predecessor, Jason Smith.

And Tina wouldn't need a referral. She was hardly the forgettable type.

Is this Charity making a covert back-channel contact? McDermitt wondered. And why? He sat down and sipped at his coffee.

Stockwell had first ordered her to return to Homestead and her cryptic reply had left them all wondering. It seemed as if she didn't trust Stockwell, for some reason. Or maybe she didn't trust the government.

Hell, after all she'd been through, it was a wonder she trusted anyone.

Travis had then ordered her to come to the Contents, knowing that Charity probably trusted him. For whatever reason, she didn't trust regular email or a phone, either.

That made sense, knowing what he knew. It was easy for the government to monitor communications and many times it was without a warrant. The only real penalty against the government for violating a person's right to privacy was that they couldn't use anything they found in court. Most of the time, the people being surveilled didn't even know their rights were violated. Stockwell had come right out and said that he had McDermitt's website monitored, to know when he chartered.

Such are the times we live in, McDermitt thought, paraphrasing his grandfather.

The door to the dock area opened and McDermitt heard Stockwell calling his name. He closed the laptop and went to the hatch, opening it.

"Yeah," McDermitt said. "In here, checking email. What's up?

"You? Checking email?" Stockwell said. "Since when?"

"Figured I'd better start, since the government spigot's about to be turned off. I'll need to charter more."

"I talked to a friend at Fort Bragg," Stockwell said, stepping over the gunwale and following McDermitt into the cabin. "An honor detail will be sent down whenever the next of kin desires. She wants a small memorial service in Montrose's backyard, but it'll be a week before she can arrange it, since she's away at college."

McDermitt opened a cupboard and took out another mug. "Thanks for doing that. You planning to be there?"

"Depends on when," Stockwell said, accepting the mug of coffee he hadn't needed to ask for. "I have to go back up to DC this week. For the next few months, I still have a job to do. I'm planning on putting my townhouse on the market." He winked and added, "Election time is a sellers' market up there."

Leaning against the island countertop, McDermitt surveyed the man over his mug. "For real this time, Colonel? You're leaving government service for good?"

Stockwell put his mug down. "Jesse, I've served in some capacity or another since two weeks after graduating high school. The only other thing I know is what I've learned down here." He picked up his mug and took a thoughtful sip of coffee. "I'm past the half-century mark. Yeah, it's time to start a new life, I think."

"I can stake you," McDermitt offered. "I mean, until your house sells. I know the government doesn't pay much."

Stockwell laughed and stood up. "I'm sure you can and would. I'm fine, though. Thirty years in the Army, most of it as a bachelor officer."

Having spent most of his own time in the Marines as a single enlisted man, McDermitt knew what Stockwell meant. Even at an enlisted man's pay, he'd managed to save quite a bit by living on base and eating at the mess hall.

"I'm going with Carl to pull lobster traps," Stockwell said. "You wanna come along?"

"No, y'all go ahead, it's my morning for a swim. Then I need to decide on whether to take a charter that just emailed."

"Carl said that'd be the case," Stockwell said, opening the hatch to the cockpit. "Take 'em out. You need something to get your mind off things."

After Stockwell left, McDermitt read the email again. To keep anyone from getting his private email, he'd had his daughter set up the website so clients could just fill in little boxes with the pertinent information. Then it generated an email to him with the name, the requested date, and any comments.

The time stamp on the email said it had been received just after midnight. He was about to reply, then thought it better to think about it a little more. What could Charity be suspicious of?

Exercise or work usually allowed him to think. The mental numbness of performing mundane physical tasks allowed his mind to wander.

Closing the laptop, McDermitt stepped down into the forward companionway and retrieved a towel from the closet. Two minutes later, he dove off the end of the pier on the north side of the island. His usual swim, three days a week, for the last four years, was around a small nearby island. It was nearly a mile away.

Born in Fort Myers, Florida, McDermitt had always lived near water and was a better-than-average swimmer. His stroke was long, aided by his six-three height. He wore only goggles and shorts on these swims, breathing steadily, and naturally, every other stroke.

Following the edge of Harbor Channel, he swam to the northeast. He knew the way without lifting his head from the water; the bottom contours, patch reefs, and turtle grass were as familiar to him as a suburbanite's backyard.

Just before reaching the deep trough carved around the little island by the tides, he stopped suddenly and stood up in waist deep water. He looked back the way he'd come, then looked all around. He was standing on the sandy bottom, which covered most of the backcountry where his island was. Only the deep channels were passable by big boats. Some others were navigable in smaller boats, but the flats were the domain of the kayak and flats skiff.

Turning, he looked off to the north of his island, where the main bunch of the Content Keys lay. He could walk there at high tide and not get his shorts wet. The only water that was deep enough for *Gaspar's Revenge* to approach his island was right next to him in Harbor Channel. That was one of the biggest factors in buying the island, nobody could get close, without being seen. He remembered Stock-well telling him that Charity was traveling in an antique sailboat. A boat like that would have a deeper draft than the *Revenge*.

"And there's no place for a deep-draft boat to go," he said aloud.

Whatever reason Charity had for her distrust wasn't appeased by offering a safe haven that could easily be construed as a trap, following the long, nearly straight channel.

McDermitt turned around and started swimming back to his island. To make up for the shorter distance, he increased his pace. If Charity was nervous about return-ing, but trusted him enough to reach out in this way, he'd do what he could to help. Being on the outside, he knew that Stockwell—and Deuce, too—had withheld truth, or just outright lied. The fact that it was to protect her or national security didn't matter very much.

An idea started forming in McDermitt's mind as his arms and legs churned steadily, a line of bubbly foam trailing behind him.

A way for him to meet Charity face-to-face, without anyone knowing, and answer any questions she might have.

CHAPTER THIRTEEN:

Waking suddenly, Charity sat up. It was already growing light out. "Victor, it's almost morning."

Reaching across him, she picked up her clothes, tossed in a pile the night before, and got dressed. She crawled out from under the makeshift tent and stretched.

Neither the camera nor the trail sensors had gone off all night. She went to the rail, hearing Victor shuffling around under the tarp. Though it was still dark, the sinking moon and stars to the west provided enough light to see their boats on the bay.

The eastern sky was starting to brighten. The mega-yacht was still there, and there were two new boats. A big sports fishing boat was at anchor near Magens Beach, and farther out toward the tip of Peterborg Peninsula a smaller charter-type boat was anchored, with a center console tied to the stern.

Victor stepped up beside her and stated the obvious. "Two new arrivals while we slept."

"I must have been tired," Charity said. "That would normally have awakened me."

The beeper on Charity's belt went off and they both looked up at the hillside. The sound reached them before they saw the source. Mopeds going downhill make a distinctive sound. Four of them appeared, coming down the far road toward the hairpin turn.

"Not them," Victor said. "Even without the scope, I can see it's two couples."

"You have an eye for the female form, huh?"

Victor turned and took Charity in his arms. "Recently? Only for one."

Charity pushed him away. "We're down to almost nothing to eat, unless we want to go back out to the boats."

"Anything fresh I had, we've eaten."

"Same here," she said.

"I have plenty of canned goods."

"Canned ham for breakfast? Ew."

"They won't strike during the day," Victor offered. "Henri lives in the next house, just down the road. Why don't I borrow his car and go into town for supplies? Anything you want in particular?"

"Steak and potatoes for dinner," she said, kissing him. "Eggs, bacon, sausage, and potatoes for breakfast. I don't eat lunch."

"Where do you put all that food?" he asked, walking toward the ladder.

"Just remember," she said, smiling brightly. "Food is energy."

He just grinned back at her and winked, before disappearing down the ladder. Charity walked over to the opposite side of the deck and stood next to the hot tub. Across the road from the house, the land dropped away precipitously into the North Atlantic Ocean. The sky grew lighter, then suddenly the bright orange crest of the sun appeared on the far horizon.

A new day, she thought, *the first day of a new life.* How easy it would be to just sail toward the rising sun, then disappear southward to the Windward Islands and beyond.

First things first, she thought. *Go home and find out what's going on. See if I'm acceptable anymore.* Turning, she went to the nest and switched off the devices to conserve power.

Fifteen minutes later, Charity stepped out onto the deck, wearing a red one-piece swimsuit. Opening the gate, she made her way down the path to the small, deserted beach, where she dropped her towel bag in her little dinghy. She went through a series of stretching exercises, flexing and shaking out her arms, loosening the joints. From her bag, she took a pair of swimmer's goggles and put them on, adjusting the fit until they were nice and snug, before wading into the water.

It was colder than she expected, less than eighty degrees, but she wasn't planning to be in it long. She waded out until the water reached mid-thigh. With the fluid grace of a former Olympic swimmer, she dove under the water. Striking out in the general direction of her boat, which lay about two hundred yards away, Charity settled into an easy, though very fast, rhythm.

Swimming, allowed her to think more clearly. It was almost as if she could put her body on autopilot, like the *Dancer,* and allow her mind to wander elsewhere. She saw no place for Charity Styles back in the real world; she'd seen too much of the evil side and not enough of the peaceful side. At the wheel of her boat, she felt peace. Swimming in tranquil, blue water relaxed her.

What would she do in the real world, take a job at a fast food place? Be a clerk at a cosmetics counter? Go back to being a Miami cop?

The real world was a world away.

Reaching *Wind Dancer*, she turned around the stern and started swimming toward Victor's boat, another two hundred yards away. She covered the distance quickly, still maintaining the same pace. As she was turning around *Salty Dog's* high bowsprit, she stopped and treaded water, looking up at the big sailing yacht. Her freeboard height was as much as a tall man, the bowsprit at least ten feet above her head. *Salty Dog* was very beamy, at least four feet wider than the *Dancer*.

Can I just leave everything behind and run off? she wondered. His boat was far more adequate for it. *Maybe after returning and finding out what's going on.*

The sound of an outboard engine caught her attention. She looked toward the sound and saw Whitaker, motoring away from his big yacht in a small dinghy. At least it was small, compared to the yacht, but it was easily twice the size of her own small inflatable. Whitaker turned and headed toward the small beach.

Oh great, she thought, remembering Lisette's warning. The last thing she wanted was to confront a naked man on a nude beach, especially one that thought he was God's gift to women.

She started a slower breaststroke, heading back to the beach, so as not to attract his attention and so she could keep an eye on him. Naked or not, he was between her and the only way to get out of the water.

His dinghy slowed as it approached the beach. She heard the engine stop and he turned around to raise it out of the water. She was still a couple of hundred yards away, with nothing above the water but her head; he didn't seem to see her, and got out to drag his dinghy higher on the sand.

Charity watched as Whitaker started immediately up the path toward the house and the road.

He must be going to meet someone, she thought, as she struck out in freestyle once more. She raised her head a few times, to see if she could see the man going up the path, but as she got closer to shore, there was less of the path to see.

Finally, Charity stood up and waded ashore, going straight for her towel bag. She quickly dried the water from her skin and wrung her hair out. She threw the strap of the bag over her head, letting the bag rest comfortably against her right hip, and started up the path. At the gate, she stopped short. Whitaker was on the deck, hands cupped around his eyes, face against the tinted French doors.

"Can I help you?" Charity said, stepping through the gate and letting it slam shut.

Whitaker wheeled, surprise on his face. "I'm sorry," he stammered. "I knocked, but nobody answered."

Charity strode toward him, cautiously. "What do you want?"

"We might have gotten off on the wrong foot," he said. He was wearing dark glasses, and Charity could feel his eyes moving up and down her body behind them. "I came to invite you to brunch."

"You do realize I'm here with Rene," she said, stepping closer, her right hand in her bag.

"I meant the both of you, of course," he countered.

Charity didn't believe that for a moment. "Thanks," she said, stepping past him, pulling the keyring from her bag, "but Rene's on his way back from town with groceries."

Whitaker took her by the elbow as she walked past. Instinctively, Charity grabbed his wrist with her free hand, dropped low, and spun under his outstretched arm. He lost his grip and she came up behind him, forcing his hand up between his shoulder blades until he was off balance. Whitaker raised his shoulder, dancing on his toes to ease the pain.

She pushed him away and planted a foot in the middle of his back, sending him sprawling into a spread-eagle belly flop in the pool.

Whitaker came up sputtering and spitting water. He spun around and started roaring with laughter. "Dammit, you got some fire!"

"Put your hand on me again, Mister Whitaker," Charity said, her right hand falling into her bag again, "and you'll learn a whole new meaning to the term."

Moving toward the steps, he came sloshing up onto the deck. "Now just a damned minute."

Reaching the deck, Whitaker started to take a step toward Charity.

Her hand came up out of the bag, the Sig in it aimed squarely at his chest.

"Whoa!" Whitaker said, taking back the half step. "Easy now."

"You're one of those guys that just can't take no for an answer, aren't you?" she shouted. "I told you I wasn't interested."

A slow grin came across Whitaker's face. "You didn't chamber a round," he said.

"A gun without a round in the chamber is no more useful than a hammer," Charity hissed, venomously. "You're here uninvited!"

The seriousness of the situation dawned on Whitaker. She was a woman alone, and he hadn't been invited. She was also quite angry—with a gun in her hand.

And he saw something else in her eyes, something beyond anger. This frightened him, and his grin faded. He suddenly realized that his being uninvited wouldn't be a case of her word against his, as had happened in the past. It would be her word against that of a corpse.

"I'm leaving," he said, slowly turning his back on her and moving toward the gate. He kept his arms above his head.

"I really did come to invite the two of you," he said over his shoulder when he stopped at the gate. "You know Mister Heureaux, and I was hoping you might help me negotiate a deal."

"You have all that money and power, and need help from a couple of boat bums to close a land deal?" Charity moved around him and, keeping the gun aimed at his chest, unlatched and swung open the gate. "Sorry, not buying any of that this week. Go back to your soulless boat."

Charity stood at the gate and followed him down the path with her eyes. A moment later, she saw his dinghy puttering back out into the bay. Turning toward the house, she put her weapon back in the bag, went inside and locked the door.

After a shower, Charity came back to the living room and sat down at Victor's computer. The email browser was still open. There were a number of emails from Yahoo, messages explaining the different features of her email account. She ignored them. There was one from an AOL account, the sender identified only as MarineVet33050. Charity recognized the numbers as the Marathon, Florida zip code. She clicked on the email and smiled.

The sound of the front door opening startled Charity and she dove for her bag on the sofa. When Victor came into the living room, he froze as he stared down the barrel of her gun.

"What happened," he asked, as Charity lowered the Sig and put it away.

Charity smiled. "Whitaker was here. I had to rough him up."

Victor's eyes rolled back, as he placed two big canvas bags on the counter in the kitchen. He turned and shook his head, as he gathered the smiling Charity into his arms. "I can't leave you for thirty minutes. What'd he want?"

"I went for a long swim and when I got back, he was looking through the back windows. He made a crude advance, then backpedaled and said he came to invite us to brunch."

Looking down at her, Victor saw Charity still smiling. "So, you kicked his ass for having the audacity to think we're the type who brunch?"

"He grabbed my arm."

"Oh." Victor accepted that as a perfectly good explanation. He remembered another time when a college man on spring break in the Caymans had grabbed her. It hadn't gone well for that guy either. "Then by all means," he said, stepping away and turning to go back out to the car, "he had it coming. I've got a couple more bags in the car."

Still smiling, she said, "Need some help?"

He stopped and studied her face. "No, I can get it. What's with the smile?"

"Jesse replied."

CHAPTER FOURTEEN:

The beeping of his watch woke Claude. He didn't know how long it had been beeping. He was tired; it could have been beeping for an hour for all he knew.

They were all tired. After loading the crates, he'd spoken at length with his transporter and they'd devised a plan.

Claude touched a button on the watch and it stopped beeping. He was hot and sweating, and the watch's digital display said it was nearly noon. The air in the small space was stale and Tarone's snoring sounded like an outboard motor.

"Wake up," Claude said, standing up and banging his head on the low ceiling. "It's time to get going."

Tarone rolled over on the opposite bunk, then stepped lightly down to the deck. "I'll get di posse up."

Claude walked through the narrow hallway and up the steps at the end. From the bridge deck, he could see that the sun was high and the sky a cloudless blue. Opening several cabinets, he found an energy bar and ate it, then sat down at the table to roll a spliff.

Half an hour later, Claude, Tarone, and seven of his best men climbed into the smaller boat. Tarone started the twin outboards. The water was calm and they weren't going far. Not that it mattered; he and all his men were equally at home on the water as they were on land.

They'd chosen their anchorage carefully. It was at the end of the peninsula, with a deep crevice large enough to hide the center console boat they were in. It only took a few minutes to get to the opening of the cleft. On Tarone's order, two men dropped small anchors over either side, letting the anchor line trail out as the boat slowly entered the gap.

When the boat's keel bumped the sandy bottom, Tarone revved the engines a second, pushing them higher on the rising bottom. The two men at the stern quickly tied off the anchor lines as two more men jumped into the water from the bow, dock lines in hand. In minutes, the little fishing boat was secure and wouldn't bounce against the rock walls on either side.

"Let's go," Claude said, jumping into the knee-deep water. He followed a little-used trail up the side of the crevice to the road, his men following behind him.

Once they were all assembled on the ridge, Claude said, "Dere are twenty-two houses on dis spit. Only nine of dem are lived in, and most of dem are renters. We start wit di first one, and move on to di next one, until we find dis mon. Remember, do not kill anyone."

The men nodded and moved off. They had an assortment of weapons, shotguns, handguns, bats, and two machine pistols.

The first house they came to was empty, but they checked it anyway. Tarone kicked in the front door and the men streamed in, going room to room. Satisfied that it was indeed unoccupied, they started down the road toward the next house.

The second house was a rental. When Tarone kicked in the door, they heard a scream, as the men all swarmed through the door. An older white woman sat on a couch in the living room, frozen in panic, as the nine black men, mostly wearing dreadlocks and dark clothing, came at her.

An old man stepped into the living room and one of Claude's men shoved him sideways onto the couch next to his wife.

"Is dere anyone else here, old man?" Tarone said, leveling a .38 revolver at his head.

The man sank back in the couch against his wife. "We're alone," he said, his voice nasally with a New England accent. "Please, take anything you want, just don't hurt us."

"Tie dere hands," Claude said, turning toward the ruined front door. "And bring dem along."

At the next house, one of the men carrying a shotgun remained on the concrete driveway with the older couple as the rest of the posse went to the house and kicked in another door. Minutes later, the men emerged, two young couples leading the way. The two men and two women all had their hands tied behind them.

"What are you people doing?" the old woman asked, as Claude passed her on the way to the next house.

Claude spun, catching the woman on the side of her face with a vicious backhand. "Yuh need to shut di hell up, old woman!"

"You can't do that!" one of the young women yelled. She was tall, with shoulder length black hair. The man she was with was taller and blond; both were dark-tanned and fit.

She took a step toward Claude, but Tarone grabbed her elbow and yanked her away from her husband and into his arms. She tried to get away, but with her hands tied tightly behind her, she could do little more than squirm.

Tarone cupped the cheeks of her ass and pulled her closer, thrusting his pelvis into hers. "We can do anyting we want, white bitch," he snarled in her face.

The tall blond man took a quick step toward them, only to have a rifle butt hit him squarely in the side of the head. The man's legs buckled, his mind already blank before his knees hit the ground. He rolled to the side and flopped onto his back, unconscious. The rifle butt opened a huge gash in his cheek, the bone visible.

Claude turned on Chris Henry. "Blood clot, mon! I and I told you don't kill nobody."

The woman Tarone was clutching screamed and broke away from him. She stumbled to her husband and fell to her knees, sobbing.

"On to di next one," Claude said, ignoring the couple and waving at the other two couples. "Take dem along."

After the group had left the driveway, Claude looked down at the sobbing woman. He could see the man's chest rising and falling and knew that he wasn't dead. "Dat yuh mon?"

She looked up, tears streaming down her face. "You didn't have to hurt him," she sobbed.

Without warning, Claude raised his silenced handgun and brought it down in a slashing motion across the woman's face. She fell beside her husband, unmoving.

He cocked his head to the side, looking at the two of them. The silencer had left a gash across her left eye and judging from the odd angle of her nose, it was broken.

"Not so pretty now, are yuh?" Claude said as he turned away.

Tarone looked over when Claude trotted up beside him. Then he glanced back at the house they'd just left. "Her ass was too skinny, anyway, Busha."

They continued down the road toward Magens Beach. Rounding a curve, they encountered a man on a bicycle. When the man saw the guns the Jamaicans were carrying, he stopped and quickly grabbed for his pants pocket. The phone was halfway up, when one of Claude's men hit it out of his hands with a baseball bat swung with great accuracy.

The man yelped and clutched his injured hand to his chest with his good one, as he tried to dismount the bike. Jacob, one of the men who had been beaten up when the Tiki bar was torched, pulled the man free of the bike and threw him to the ground. In seconds, his hands were tied and he was lifted to his feet.

"Don't say nutin," Jacob said. "Not one word, mon. Go wit di udders or be killed."

The next two houses were empty. It being the slow season for tourists, this was to be expected. In the next house, they found the bicycler's wife and teenage son, tied their hands, and marched them on down the road with the growing group of bound captives.

Rounding a curve in the road, Claude saw a car pull into a driveway at the top of the hill. He didn't think the driver saw them, though. The rest of his men and their captives were well behind him.

Just ahead was another driveway, a hundred feet before the one the car had pulled into. A car was a sure sign of a local, not a tourist. Golf carts and scooters were the preferred transportation for visitors. They'd have to be more careful at that house. Tourists were rarely armed, but a lot of the locals could have guns.

As Claude marched down the next driveway, two men stayed behind to control the group. The others hurried to catch up.

"Can I help you?" a voice asked.

Claude spun around and brought his gun up. A tall, slim, black man with close-cropped gray hair and amber eyes stood next to some shrubs. He'd been hidden behind them, and as yet hadn't seen the others.

"Come out from dere," Claude said. One of his men veered away and grabbed the old man's arms from behind.

"What are you doing?" the man shouted, trying to pull his arms away. He somehow got free, wheeled, and pointed a long pair of pruning shears menacingly at the man who had grabbed him.

The man who'd grabbed him raised a revolver and pointed it at the man's head. "Yuh don't bring scissors to a gunfight, old fool."

The rest of Claude's men came into view, along with the captives. The man with amber eyes suddenly turned his head and shouted, "Lisette, call the police!"

Tarone and three others broke from the group and ran to the house, crashing through the door without even trying the knob. There were shouts and a scream from inside. This diverted the old man's attention long enough for two men to rush him and take him to the ground. A moment later, a short old woman was brought out of the house, her hands tied behind her back.

"She had di phone in her hand," Tarone said, shoving her toward her husband. "But, she never made di call."

Claude nodded up the hill. "A car just pulled into di next house," he said. "Prob'ly a local. Have two men keep di prisoners back, while we sneak up to di door."

Tarone relayed the orders and two men, one with the shotgun and another with a ball bat, stayed with the group as Claude led the others forward.

The sides of the road offered some cover in the way of large rocks, palm trees, cactus, and shrubs. The men quickly reached the driveway, and Claude peeked around the hedge that fronted the width of the yard. He quickly drew his head back.

"One mon," he whispered. "Just coming out of di house. Di car trunk is open. Get ready."

Peering through the hedge, Claude watched as the man went to the back of the car. When his back was turned, Claude motioned his men forward quickly. Their footfalls on the concrete must have alerted the man just as he lifted a second canvas bag out of the car's trunk.

With Claude's men only ten feet away, the man dropped the bags and turned around, a gun coming up from his waistband. Tarone reached him first, planting a shoulder in the man's belly and driving him back against the car. The gun fell to the ground as the two men started wrestling to get control. Two more of Claude's men grabbed the white man and dragged the two apart.

Tarone was quickly on his feet. "Hold him!" he growled.

With the two men holding him, Tarone punched him hard in the mid-section. The air whooshed from the man's lungs. When he reflexively bent forward, Tarone grabbed his hair and lifted his face, bringing the barrel of his revolver down against the side of his head. The man sagged, blood running freely from a gash above his left eye.

"Tie dis one up, too," Claude said, moving toward the open front door.

Tarone and the rest of the men joined him and they went straight through the door like they owned the place. When they entered the main room of the house, a blond woman stood at the back door looking out over the deck behind the house. She heard them and turned.

As Jacob moved toward her, the woman lunged for a bag on the sofa. Tarone stepped to the side and was at the bag before she could reach it. When he snatched it up, she simply stopped, hands hanging at her side, a blank expression on her face.

Too late, Jacob recognized her. His hands were already reaching to grab the woman's shoulders when he realized she was the same woman who had intervened at the Tiki bar.

With blinding speed, the woman spun away from Jacob's outstretched hands. Claude watched, amazed, as she continued her spin and raised her elbow, never taking her eyes off Tarone, before snapping her head around like a ballerina, striking Jacob on the back of the neck with her elbow, and again making eye contact with Tarone.

Jacob went down in a heap on the sofa, unmoving. Tarone kicked the table out of the way as Chris Henry charged the woman, his bat raised high. Tarone feinted with a left jab, then followed with a roundhouse right that would have taken almost any man down. The woman's reflexes were faster, though. She ignored the left, catching his right wrist in both hands and spinning with it.

Chris's bat came down on Tarone's shoulder and his momentum carried him stumbling past the two, only to be swept into the glass door by Tarone's flying body. The French door's muntins splintered, the glass panes shattering as the two men fell through it in a heap, landing on the concrete deck outside.

Claude aimed his silenced pistol at the ceiling above the woman's head and fired. The bullet's impact with the plaster made more sound than the gunshot.

Dust fell on the woman and she turned quickly to face him, her hair whipping across a grim, determined face and maniacal eyes. In an instant, the woman's expression changed to one of compliance as she raised her hands.

With Claude's gun on the woman, the remaining two men moved to get behind her.

Outside, Tarone struggled to his feet, his left hand clutching his injured right shoulder. Stumbling sideways, he stepped on Chris's bat and nearly went down. Chris was slowly coming up to his hands and knees, his right arm dripping blood from a severe gash.

Tarone gripped the bat in his left hand and came up with it high over his head. Before anyone could say or do anything, the bat came down hard on Chris's head and he collapsed to the ground, feet twitching. Tarone pummeled him repeatedly with the bat, until blood and brain tissue were splashed all over the white concrete.

Tossing the bloody bat aside, Tarone clutched his injured shoulder and kicked Chris's corpse in the ribs, then turned and stumbled toward the shattered door.

The two men had tied the woman's hands behind her back and each held her firmly by the arms. Tarone stalked toward her, his face a mask of rage.

"Tarone!" Claude shouted. "Not so fast, mon."

Claude's second-in-command ignored him as he moved toward the woman, left fist clenched and already coming back.

Suddenly, the woman went limp in the men's hands. Both thinking she'd fainted or something, they held her tighter, lifting her up for the beating they knew Tarone was about to administer.

Tarone never saw her feet move until it was too late. With the men holding her up, she raised both legs, curling her body up, and kicked Tarone so hard in the face with her bare feet that the impact lifted him off the ground.

The force of the kick caused the two men holding her to stumble backward and they both tripped over the coffee table, releasing the woman. She landed on her feet, almost cat-like, and slowly turned, looking at the five men sprawled around her, then up at Claude.

"Bring dem all inside!" Claude shouted, his pistol still aimed at the woman. "If yuh move one more time," he told her. "I will shoot you. Now go outside."

The two men who had been holding the woman struggled to their feet and followed Claude, as he followed the woman through the broken door. She stepped over the gruesome corpse and didn't seem to notice it.

"Dat's far enough," Claude said. One by one, the captives stepped out onto the deck, several turning their heads away from Chris's body. The older woman retched and hid her face.

"Line dem up behind dat bitch," Claude said. "Cept di grocery man. Put him beside her."

Two men with machine pistols crowded the captives together behind the man and woman, as Claude stepped slowly toward them. Tarone somehow managed to get back on his feet and fell groggily through the door.

"You okay, Tarone?" Claude asked, as the man stepped up beside him, shaking off the effects of the kick.

Rolling his shoulder, Tarone said, "Give me half an hour with her, Busha. I and I teach her a good lesson."

"Search di house, mon," Claude said. "I tink we found di man dat was shooting at us."

Tarone pointed to two men and led them inside. A moment later, Jacob came out. He had Tarone's big revolver.

"Tarone say to help yuh," Jacob said.

"Point yuh gun at dat woman's head," Claude said, pointing at the blonde. "If she moves, kill her."

When Jacob was in position, Claude stepped up to the tall man. The open wound above his eye still pulsed, and with each throb, more blood ran down the side of his face.

"Dis yuh woman?" Claude asked, nodding his head sideways.

The man didn't answer. He just stared into Claude's eyes, hatred building in his own.

Claude turned to the woman. "Dis yuh mon?"

She slowly turned and looked at Claude, her breathing still a little ragged. Then she turned and looked at the man standing beside her. She seemed to study his features for a moment before she turned back to face Claude.

"Yes," she replied.

Turning back to the tall, sandy-haired man, Claude opened his mouth to say something, when Tarone came back out onto the deck, carrying what looked like a black assault rifle with a scope.

"Dis was on di roof," Tarone said. "Dis scope has night time optics."

Claude turned back toward the man. "It was you dat made di tree branch fall on me." It wasn't a question—more like an accusation.

Without warning, Claude's left hand shot out, his fist connecting with the man's face with a sickening smack. The man stumbled backward but stayed on his feet. One of the women behind him screamed.

"Yuh evah hear di name Claude Whyte?" he asked, fists up and dancing around the man's left side. "I was di best fighter on di Jamaican boxing team. Now I gwon give you a little show." Claude stopped dancing as the man regained his footing and stood steadily again, a small cut over his right eye. "Why yuh shooting at us? Who yuh work for."

The blonde's mouth opened as if to speak, but Claude drew his gun and pointed it right between her eyes.

"I and I not ask yuh a thing, bitch. Now watch careful and I teach yuh man to box." He then pointed to the teenage son of the bicycler and said to Jacob, "If she opens her mouth, shoot dat white boy."

Putting his gun away, Claude again started to dance around the tall man. "Dat punch I hit yuh wit? Dat was a left jab." In an instant, Claude's footing changed, leading with the right. In a blur, his right fist shot out, glancing off the man's head, as he barely moved in time to escape the full force of the blow.

Still, it rocked him backward.

"Dat right dere," Claude said, smiling and dancing away. "Right jab."

Suddenly, Claude stepped forward with his right foot, his left arm arcing over his shoulder. His fist connected with the defenseless man's head, right where the cut had started to appear. The man stumbled sideways, his head leading the way toward the ground.

"Whoo!" Claude shouted gleefully, as he danced away again. "Overhand left! Bet yuh didn't see dat one coming."

The man went down to one knee, but Claude was on him again, bunching the man's tee-shirt in his fist and hoisting him back to his feet.

"See, mon," Claude said, speaking to the captives, "dis is just what yuh need protection from."

He punched the man twice with his right fist, holding him up with his left. Then he let the man drop and turned to the other captives. A pool of blood began to spread around the man's face.

"Don't know if yuh are tourists visitin' here," he snarled at the prisoners. "Or if yuh own dese houses. It don't matter." He walked over to the group and got right up in the face of the young woman, whose friends he'd left bleeding in the driveway. "Yuh two friends back dere at di house? Dey both gwon need a plastic surgeon now."

The dark-haired woman had tears streaming down her face.

Claude grinned down at her, then stepped back and addressed them all. "If I and I don't get my protection money ... well, shit like dis gwon happen all di time."

"Please stop," the old man with the amber eyes pleaded. "We'll pay you what you want. All of us."

Claude stepped over in front of the tall black man and looked deep into his eyes. "Yuh know what, old mon," he said slowly. "I almost believe yuh. Almost." He stepped around in front of the blond woman again. "Whadayuh tink 'bout yuh man now?"

She looked slowly over to where the man lay unconscious and bleeding, then her eyes came back to Claude. She didn't blink; her expression was completely devoid of emotion. There was no trembling, no heaving sobs. Her eyes seemed to burn right through Claude. They practically sparkled with intensity.

The sparkle didn't come from tears, though. What Claude saw in her eyes was disconcerting. She was a pretty woman, even beautiful—a bit taller than Claude liked, but well put together. Her face was tan, her skin smooth and flawless, but in her eyes, he saw evil.

"I'm going to kill you," the woman said quietly.

"Is dat right?" Claude sneered. Then he turned and went back to the man lying in his own blood. "Pick dat meat bag up," he ordered the two biggest of his men.

Together, they hauled the white man up to his feet. His legs refused to support his body and he sagged forward. Claude's right fist came crashing down on the side of the man's face, blood and what appeared to be a couple of teeth spraying onto the deck from the blow.

Claude nodded at the two men and they dropped the unconscious man to the ground.

"Take her," Claude said, pointing at the blonde. Then he walked over to the tall black man with the short round wife. "Twenty-two houses, old mon," he began. "And four businesses." Then he grinned. "Sorry, dat's three businesses since dat terrible fire. At five hundred a month each,

I need yuh to bring me twelve-thousand-five-hundred dollars by tomorrow. Any cops come snoopin' 'round, di woman dies."

Without waiting for a reply, Claude turned and marched into the house, the two big men following and shoving the woman ahead of them.

CHAPTER FIFTEEN:

Hearing voices, Victor tried to open his eyes. The effort hurt, and he lapsed back into blackness, but not before his mind registered one of the voices as the rich mega-yacht owner.

Later—he had no idea how much later—he felt something cool and damp against his forehead, and moaned.

"I think he is waking up," he heard Lisette say.

One eye opened slightly. The room was dark. Several faces, or maybe just one, hovered sideways in front of his face. Soon, more appeared, all fuzzy and distorted, moving like the bits of glass in a kaleidoscope.

Gradually the many images resolved into three black faces. It startled Victor and he tried to push them away. But blankets were piled over him. Blinking his one good eye, he recognized his friends, Henri, Lisette, and Chet.

"Charity," Victor moaned, as his head fell back onto the pillow.

"Nonsense, Rene," Henri said, smiling down at him. "I'm not a man to give handouts and you're not the kind to take any." Then, to Lisette, he said, "I think he's delusional."

"No," Victor said. "Gabby? Where is she?"

"The Jamaicans took her," Henri replied, his face a mask of concern. "But I will get her back in the morning. I'm going to pay the protection money and get her back."

"The police?" Victor asked, trying to push the covers off. "Help me up, Chet."

"No," Lisette said, stepping closer and putting a hand on his shoulder. "You need to rest. I've only just got the bleeding to stop. You need a doctor."

"I need to get to my boat," Victor said, pushing past her, and sitting up. His head spun for a moment. He gingerly put a hand to his face, wincing at the touch.

"The police came," Chet said. "Mister Whitaker and me convinced the young couple to not mention the dead man on the patio. Their two friends needed a doctor, so the youngsters told the police it was a break in. The others went along, in deference to Mister Whitaker. He offered to pay for everything."

"I have to find out where they took her," Victor said, as Chet helped him get unsteadily to his feet.

"Please, Rene," Henri said. "We know you are on the run from something, but, we know you're a good man. That's why we didn't say anything to the police about you, Gabriella, or their own man who they killed here. Let me handle this. I'll pay them what they want."

Victor stood straight and turned to his friend, fixing him hard with his one eye. "No, Henri. People like them, they never stop. They just keep coming and coming. I'll see that they get paid exactly what they deserve. If I can find them."

Taking the first tentative step toward the bedroom door, he knew that if he could just get outside, get out under the stars, he'd be okay. The others followed as he made his way through the wrecked living room and out the back door.

The dead man lay in a massive pool of blood, his head beaten to a pulp. "Chet," Victor whispered, pulling the old man aside. "Can you clean that up? Do something with the body?"

"It'll be shark shit before the sun rises," the old man said, a bit of a sparkle in his dark brown eyes. "Those men? They're staying in one of the smaller houses at Estate Canaan. The blue one."

It hurt to smile, but Victor did anyway. "How do you know this, old friend?"

Chet shrugged. "It's a small island. You know the house?"

Victor gripped Chet's shoulder. "Yes, very well."

Taking two steps toward the back gate, Victor stopped and turned around, a puzzled look on his battered face. "Whitaker was here?"

"He heard the commotion and came to investigate," Lisette said. "If he'd been a minute sooner, he'd have been in the same mess and we would probably all still be tied up."

Victor turned and looked out at the big boat on the bay. It dwarfed his and Charity's boats combined. Lights spilled out onto the decks and the water all around it was illuminated by underwater lights.

"Where is he now?"

Henri stepped toward him. "He went with the two couples from up the road. To make sure the injured receive good medical attention."

Victor nodded. "Gabby and I will be back later tonight. Then I think we'll probably be leaving."

Turning, Victor went to the gate and down the path to the beach. He'd been right. Just getting out of the confined space of that bedroom, breathing the fresh salty air, he felt better. And his other eye was now partly open.

On the beach, he untied his dinghy and shoved it to deeper water. He climbed in, fixed the oars in the locks, and started rowing. He kept close to the shoreline as he rowed the length of Little Magens Beach. Then he turned and, keeping Charity's boat between him and the large yacht, rowed hard toward *Salty Dog*.

Before climbing aboard, he edged the dinghy around the high stern while standing on the helm seat. He saw no movement on the yacht, but there were two tenders tied to the stern, one a large rigid inflatable and the other the twin-engine center console he'd seen the crew depart in the day before.

The crew must be back aboard, Victor thought, *and apparently Whitaker didn't go to the hospital with the others.*

He was sure the RIB was the millionaire's dinghy. Victor didn't know why he thought he needed to be stealthy, but both he and Charity had agreed the rich developer was a little odd.

He climbed aboard and went quickly down into the cabin. In the forward head, Victor looked at his reflection in the mirror. It was bad, but he'd seen worse. Trouble was, it was usually the other guy who'd looked worse.

The bigger gash over his left eye would need stitches, or it would pull open again—so he stitched it. Not an easy task to do in a mirror, particularly when the needle got slippery with blood. He finished it up, then bandaged the wound. He put several butterfly bandages on the other cut, cleaned up his face as best he could, and went to the master stateroom for a clean shirt.

Back in the pilothouse, Victor looked aft, toward Charity's sloop, the mega-yacht behind it, and the open Atlantic beyond that. He'd come to Magens Bay to see old friends and relax in a place he felt comfortable and safe. He never stayed long in any one place, and had only been planning to stay a few days. It had already been that long, and he was now wrapped up in something that could easily expose him.

He stood at the lower helm for a moment, indecisive, looking ahead toward the beach and aft to the sea. He could start the big diesel in the engine room just below the bridge deck, flip a switch and hoist the anchor, then point the bow toward open water. In a matter of minutes, he could disappear. Like smoke.

That was exactly what he should do—and he would have, had it not been for Charity. He couldn't understand why she mattered. He'd disappeared on more than one woman when the authorities had gotten too close. Emotional attachments were for other people.

But he felt different about this one. She was like him.

Instead, Victor opened a cabinet beside the helm, then reached up inside it and released a catch that dropped a false panel down. He'd built a number of hiding places like this into the boat's interior, and up in the cockpit. From this hiding place, he removed six small cylinders, each about four inches long and two across. He placed each one on the counter, then went down to his aft stateroom.

Moments later, Victor emerged, a black tactical pack over one shoulder and a long slender bag over the other. He stuffed the cylinders into the pack, leaving it and the long bag in the wheelhouse. He went down the forward steps to the salon, and when he emerged from there he was carrying a second black backpack.

Minutes later, Victor was over the side and untying the dinghy's painter. Again, he chose the oars over the engine and retraced his route to the little beach below the house. Tying his skiff in the same spot, he looked back at the yacht anchored behind his and Charity's boats. The lights were still on, flooding the interior and spilling out onto the water. He saw movement on the bridge deck, but it was too far away to tell who it was. The two smaller boats were still tied to the stern.

As he climbed the steep path to the house, Victor's head throbbed with every step. Finally, he reached the deck. The lights were all turned off and nobody was around. The body was gone, as well. The spot where it had been was wet with water. As Victor walked around the pool, toward the broken door, a small figure stepped out of the shadows.

Victor wasn't surprised. "Where's the body?"

"Being loaded onto my boat about now, I'd expect. My brother is going fishing tonight."

"I can't take you with me, Chet."

The older man scratched absently at an eyebrow. "If you don't, I'll only get there late and probably be of no use."

Victor studied the older man's features. He knew Chet would follow on his own, even if told not to. "Would you believe me if I told you I debated hoisting anchor and taking off?"

"Yes, and yet here we both are," Chet replied. "I've seen how you look at her, Rene. I owe you much more than this. At least use me to create a diversion."

Victor shrugged the backpack off, and set it on the deck, along with the long bag. "Put these in the car. I have to get a few other things here."

Disappearing into the house, Victor quickly went to the places he and Charity had stashed weapons and collected them. Then he climbed up the ladder to the roof, to see if the Jamaicans had taken everything. He found the spotting scope, camera, and laptop just where they'd left them, but the rifle was gone.

He swiped a finger across the mouse pad, and the computer came alive. It was still on the program to operate the sensors. He quickly activated the sensors and put both the laptop and scope into his bag along with the guns.

Once outside, Victor put the bag in the backseat where Chet had already put the rest of the equipment. He tossed the keys to his friend.

"You drive," Victor said, as he went around to the passenger side. "We have one stop to make. Halfway up the hill from the sharp turn."

Minutes later, Chet negotiated the old Mercedes around the sharp turn with practiced ease, then accelerated smoothly up through the gears.

"Pull over," Victor said, when they'd reached the spot where the motion sensors were hidden.

Once Chet brought the old car to a stop, Victor got out. He quickly disappeared down the hill on the side of the road, trusting his memory on where he and Charity had put the sensors. Minutes later, he returned and put the small devices into one of the packs, then got back in the front seat.

"You know William Waters, right?" Victor asked.

Chet nodded as he put the car into gear and started up the hill once more. "He's not on the island," Chet replied.

"I want you to drop me off at his house," Victor said, handing one of his throwaway handguns to the older man. "Then wait there at the house for thirty minutes. After that, I want you to go on up and around to Estate Canaan. Think you can hit the electric transformer on the pole without hitting the house?"

Chet nodded again, as the car accelerated through the pass and started down the other side.

"Do that, then get out of there," Victor said. "Empty the magazine into it and don't wait around. Just go back to William's house and wait for us."

"The man said he would kill her," Chet said quietly, as he turned off the main road.

"He won't," Victor said. "She's his only bargaining chip. Once they realize you're not the cops, I'll be inside."

"And if they don't all come out to the front?"

"I'll kill them," Victor replied, matter-of-factly.

Chet only nodded. They drove on in silence and after a few minutes, Chet turned off the road onto a steep drive-way. The concrete drive turned and ended behind a small house, the front of which sat high on stilts.

Victor got out of the car without a word, opened the back door, and gathered up the two packs and the long bag. He unzipped the bag and removed a fully automatic M-16 rifle. Mounted just below the barrel was a sinister looking M-203 grenade launcher.

"Be careful, my friend," Chet said, as Victor inserted a magazine in the rifle and chambered a round.

"You do the same," Victor replied, before tossing the bag back into the car and shouldering the rifle. "Remember, wait here for thirty minutes. That'll give me time to get into position. Then we'll meet you back here in one hour."

Victor disappeared into the woods behind the house. In the darkness, he opened one of the packs, took out an old pair of starlight goggles, and gingerly pulled the straps over his head. After switching on the optics, it took a moment to get used to the gray-green surroundings they illuminated.

There was a tiny infrared light mounted between the two optical barrels, which he also activated. Suddenly, the terrain around him was lit up, like a powerful spotlight was mounted on his head. The tiny light would be invisible without the aid of the light intensifying optics, but gave depth and texture to his immediate surroundings.

Moving quickly but quietly, Victor made his way up the hill, pausing every twenty or thirty feet to look ahead and listen. As he grew nearer to the house on the hill, he began to hear reggae music coming from above.

The back of the blue house faced Magens Bay, far below. Like William's house, this one was on stilts, the rear deck twenty feet above the backyard. Through the trees, Victor saw two sets of stairs descending from the deck's corners, meeting at a small landing, with a single set of stairs going from there to the ground. Below the steps, there was at least thirty feet of open lawn, sloping gently to the tree line. The trees themselves had been used as a sort of buttress, holding back the fill dirt, rocks, and debris that had been dumped to create a gently sloping lawn. The fill and debris spilled between them and down the steep hillside.

A lot of time in the open, he thought, as he studied the house from a safe distance.

Removing the laptop from the first bag, Victor placed it on a fallen log, but left it closed. From a pocket on the pack, he pulled out a miniature infrared beacon, similar to the tiny light on the goggles. He attached the flashing beacon to a tree branch above the computer and activated it. The light would flash every three seconds and would also be invisible to the naked eye. But with his starlight goggles, it would provide him an easy target to run toward, if things got hairy.

Taking the second pack and moving as fast as he could without making noise, Victor went further up the hill, angling toward the corner of the property to his right. Reaching the spot where fill and debris cascaded down from the two sides of the yard, he paused and studied the clearing from a different angle.

Not seeing anyone, he climbed the steeper debris pile to the edge of where the trees gave way to the yard. Moving in a line running parallel to the back of the house, but well inside the buttressing trees, Victor mounted five motion sensors to five equally spaced trees. Once he got Charity out, they could move down the hill to the beacon, where the rest of the gear was stashed. If anyone came down the steps and into the woods, the computer would show where they were.

Satisfied that he'd taken every precaution he could, for a fast and safe extraction, Victor moved back to the center of the property and cautiously approached the edge of the clearing. Looking around, he found several trees that were close enough together that the debris from creating the backyard spilled around them and stacked up on the other side well above his head.

One of the trees in the middle was obviously dead. Kneeling beside it, Victor looked down the hill for the strobe. When it flashed, he could see that there was nothing blocking his view. He started digging between the trees, pulling out rotted logs, rocks, and dirt, as quietly as possible. From the pack, he removed three sticks of dynamite bundled together and gently placed them in the crevice. Removing a second strobe from the pack, he placed it directly in front of the dynamite, making sure that it was nowhere near being in contact.

Satisfied, he went around the large debris pile and worked his way up above it to the edge of the yard. There, he pushed the starlight goggles up onto his forehead, switching them off to save energy. The bottom of the steps was only ten yards across open grass, all of it well-lit from lights on the deck.

For now.

Crouched behind a large boulder, Victor waited. He could hear voices above, muffled as if they were inside the house. He couldn't make out what was being said, but he was certain that it was several men talking.

Victor quietly opened the pack and removed the six canisters. Two were marked M651. He put one of those in his left cargo pocket and quietly slid the barrel grip of the grenade launcher forward. He opened the second canister and inserted the CS grenade it contained into the breach, sliding the grip back into place, cocking the launcher.

The other four canisters, all marked M381, he put in his right cargo pocket. He knew without checking that all the guns in his pack were loaded, with rounds chambered.

Suddenly, he heard six rapid booms, coming from above, as the lights on the deck went off.

Victor switched the starlight goggles back on, and gingerly lowered them over his eyes. He stepped out from behind the boulder and aimed the launcher at the top of the large center window at the back of the now darkened house. He fired the launcher, which made a hollow popping sound and quickly loaded the second tear-gas grenade in the launcher, as he heard the satisfying sound of glass breaking. He closed the breach, aimed, and fired again.

Without waiting, Victor sprinted across the clearing, eyes on the deck above, as the crash of another broken window could be heard, along with a lot of shouting and coughing.

Through the night vision optics, he saw nobody moving on the deck, but he could hear plenty of muffled shouts from inside the house. Two minutes was all he needed. He had a gas mask in the pack, but it was impossible to wear it and the starlight goggles at the same time. He'd tried. If he couldn't find her in two minutes, he'd have to take the goggles off and put on the mask to breathe.

That would create a lot more problems. He'd be in the dark along with his adversaries, and he wasn't even sure the mask would seal to his battered face.

He'd brought it for Charity to use.

CHAPTER SIXTEEN:

The bindings dug into Charity's wrists as she struggled to get loose, careful to move only her hands—and only when nobody was looking. As they left the villa, Charity soon realized why the motion sensors hadn't alerted her. Instead of going toward the mainland, the men trudged toward the end of the peninsula, pushing and shoving her ahead of them.

On the steep trail down the cliff, she stumbled and nearly fell over the edge. She scraped a knee on the rough rock and could feel blood slowly inching down her shin. Once they reached the bottom, two men forced her onto a small boat and held her jammed against the deck in the forward part of the boat, forcing a hood of some kind over her head.

She couldn't see where they were going, but before they covered her head, Charity saw all the legal sizes of gamefish she might be able to catch, each identified on a long sticker on the inside of the hull. Someone had written *It's only illegal if you get caught* on the corner of the narrow Department of Natural Resources sign.

Thank you, illegal fisherman, she thought, as she rubbed her skinned knee against a rough piece of trim around a rod holder.

Over the twin outboards, Charity recognized the voice of the man she'd thrown through the French door. "When we gwon take di udder million dollars to di transport boat, Busha?"

The leader of the group replied, his voice low so Charity couldn't hear, but she heard anyway. "Dere's di boat cap'n, now. Before he takes dis boat back, bring di box of money out and give it to him. Dey have plenty room on dat big launch deck."

The sound of big diesel engines starting close by drowned out anything else they said. Charity knew they hadn't gone far, certainly not out of the bay, but it was impossible to tell which way they'd gone. The small boat slowed and she felt it bump something. The smell and sound of the rumbling diesel engines told Charity that it had to be one of the big sport fishing boats they'd seen. Rough hands grabbed at her and hauled her to her feet.

Charity didn't resist. It would be futile against perhaps a dozen armed men. More hands grabbed her and pulled her over the boat's gunwale and up onto the larger boat.

She was forced down into the boat's cabin, but not before she heard a different voice, with a distinct Texas accent. "What the hell'd you bring her for and what's with another crate?"

Committing the man's voice to memory, Charity allowed someone to steer her forward. "Stop," the man behind her said. "Feel forward wit yuh feet, dere's three steps down."

A moment later, she was locked in a little cabin and she could hear the boat they'd arrived on speed away. She also heard an electric windlass and the rattle of the anchor chain. They were going somewhere.

The boat ride was short, less than an hour. She felt the boat bump against something, probably a dock. The engines were shut down and after quite a while, Charity was taken off the boat and forced into the back of a van, which was parked just a few steps from the boat. The drive was short, with several sharp turns. Charity calculated that they weren't very far from the villa, probably still on the island.

She was taken from the van and marched into a house. Once inside, she was guided and shoved this way and that, and finally pushed down onto a very small bed. She heard the door close and lock. Even without seeing, she could tell it was a tiny room, probably a baby's nursery.

Over the course of the next few hours, about every ten minutes or so, someone opened the door for a moment, then closed it without saying a word. After each visit, she worked on the bindings around her wrists.

Hearing footsteps on the tile floor, Charity quickly rolled onto the bed, her back to the wall, assuming as close as possible the position she'd been in before.

Again, the door opened. This time, it stayed open a little longer than before. Though the hood blocked any light, she felt the man's eyes crawling all over her. With the passing of each microsecond, the demons in her mind pushed their door open a little more. Anger and hatred began to build and Charity had to focus to force them back down. Exploding in a fit of rage would accomplish nothing, but to get her hurt. Or worse.

When the door finally closed again, Charity immediately swung her feet to the floor and squatted beside the bed. She began working the restraints against the bed rail again, trying desperately to pull the bindings down over her wrists. She worked furiously, ignoring the pain it caused, knowing that the next time the man opened the door his visit was going to be a lot longer. She felt certain it was the same man who'd beaten the other man's brains out at the villa. The same man she'd thrown through the door and then kicked in the face.

From the sound of their voices, the men in the next room were drinking and playing some sort of card or board game, occasionally laughing at or cursing one another.

Just as Charity felt the thin rope beginning to give and slide over her blood-lubricated wrists, she heard the distinct sound of gunfire, coming from outside the house.

Chairs scraped and men shouted, then Charity's hands were suddenly free. She pulled the hood off, surprised to see that the room was nearly dark; the only light was from the moon streaming through the window. She went to the door and listened a moment. No light spilled under the crack at the bottom of the door, either.

Just as she was about to crack the door open, she heard the sound of breaking glass, followed by a loud pop. A couple of seconds passed, and she heard another window breaking in the room on the other side of where she was.

The voices beyond the door started to sound panicked, as men began to cough and run toward the part of the house they'd come in from. She assumed it was the front, the same direction she'd heard the gunshots.

A whiff of tear gas reached her nose. She dove toward the bed and buried her face in the soft cotton comforter, taking a deep breath. Holding it, she quickly gathered up the hood that had been over her head, doubled it and covered her mouth with it. It wouldn't block all the gas, but it would lessen the effect.

Just as she reached for the door, it flew open and the man she'd thrown through the French door at the villa stood in front of her.

"Yuh loose, now? Dat's good," he said, leering at her through tear-filled eyes. "Time I teach yuh dat lesson."

He came at her then, moving quickly to gain a stranglehold. Charity let him. As his fingers encircled her throat, she stepped back, pulling him off-balance. She brought both hands up and over his outstretched arms, forcing them down, as she stepped back further.

Though he was stronger than her, it didn't matter in Charity's way of fighting. The Israeli fighting technique she'd learned and perfected went beyond most. Krav Maga holds and strikes were designed to be lethal, not just to incapacitate. He was off-balance and his arms fully outstretched. She grabbed his thumbs and twisted them up and then outward, feeling and hearing the tendons tear.

Losing his grip, the man countered with a wild right hand, a punch meant to knock down or even kill a smaller opponent such as herself. She easily swayed backward, swatting the punch aside. Charity wanted a jab.

When the man regained his balance, he grinned and gave her just what she wanted, a straight right jab to the face. Turning away from the punch, she caught the man's wrist and again pulled him off balance. His head dipped as he tried to regain his footing, and Charity brought her right elbow down hard on the back of his neck while pulling his outstretched right arm further toward her, barring it in place on her shoulder.

With her right elbow on the back of the man's neck, she locked her hand under his outstretched arm, applying even more leverage.

Completely off balance now, the man went down to his knees, as Charity applied greater and greater force, pushing his head down toward his chest and forcing his right arm even higher. Just as his head was about to crash against the floor, she felt the crack.

The man's whole body went limp, dropping to the floor with a thud, his head turned at an unusual angle.

Grabbing the hood again, she pressed it to her face, tears already running freely from her eyes. During the struggle, she'd managed to hold her breath. She finally exhaled and took another deep breath through the hood's cloth.

She could taste the gas, and resisted the urge to gag and cough. It wasn't the first time she'd breathed CS gas.

Charity released the dead man and patted him on the back. "You just keep teaching those lessons," she mumbled through the hood.

Grabbing one of the dead man's legs, she dragged the body away from the door and quickly searched him. She found a big Colt handgun and hefted it in her hand. In the dim moonlight spilling through the window, she pulled the slide back to check that there was a round in the chamber, and released it. She quickly released the magazine and looked at the view ports. Four rounds.

Through the window, Charity could see that there was no way out that way. It was at least twenty feet down to the ground outside. She returned to the door. The shouting and coughing were still going on, but more muffled. She cracked the door and looked out. She only had a few seconds left, before the gas would permeate the cloth. Tears were already streaming down her cheeks, making it difficult to see.

Blinking several times to clear her eyes, she threw the door open and stepped out into a well-appointed living room, full of thick white smoke.

The gunshots had come from the front of the house, and that was where she heard the men shouting. There was broken glass by the back door. A smoking gas grenade hissed its last breath on the floor, then fell silent. Realizing the gunshots were a diversion, she started toward the back of the house, toward whoever had fired the CS grenade.

Hearing a shout from the front of the house, much closer and inside the door, Charity dropped beside a sofa, the heavier gas in the room stinging her eyes. The urge to cough was overwhelming. Her experience told her not to, that coughing would only make it worse. When she looked over the top of the couch, two men were coming through the open door.

Charity opened her own door, the one in her mind that she usually kept locked tight. Letting the flood of hostility and rage spring forth, she harnessed and directed it. She rose from behind the sofa and moved toward the approaching men, firing a round with every footfall. The gas was dissipating and all the men were charging back into the house, apparently realizing the gunshots out front had been a diversion.

The first four men through the door went down. As more streamed in behind them, the slide on Charity's gun locked to the rear and she tossed it aside. She waded into the approaching men, feet and fists flying. Two more went down, then someone grabbed her around the waist from behind. She bent forward, grabbing a wrist, and rolling the man over her hip. When he hit the ground on his back, her bare foot came down hard on his throat, crushing his windpipe.

Charity heard a spitting sound and felt a tug at her shoulder. Spinning, she saw the leader of the group; in his hand was a large-caliber suppressed handgun pointed directly at her. She calculated the distance instinctively, and just as she was about to launch herself at the man, there was a crash of breaking glass behind her. The man turned toward the sound.

Looking over her shoulder, Charity saw Victor rolling across the floor. He came up in a kneeling position, his face hidden behind an old-style pair of starlight goggles. He leveled an assault rifle at the man and flames spat from the muzzle as he fired a three-round burst.

The leader dove behind an overstuffed recliner and Victor fired another burst into the chair, then turned and fired a longer burst toward the front of the house.

"Here!" Victor shouted, swinging a pack off his shoulder and reaching inside. He tossed a handgun to her; when she caught it she instantly recognized her own Sig.

The gas was slowly being blown out of the house by the ocean breeze coming through the shattered back door. The light wind carried it through the open front door, but it was still thick, choking and gagging her, stinging her eyes.

She dropped behind the couch next to Victor, and he took a Vietnam-era gas mask from the pack and handed it to her. Charity quickly pulled it on and tightened the straps. She cleared it and checked the seal, then brought her Sig back up.

Taking turns, they each fired several volleys at the front door, and Victor also fired a few rounds at the chair, unsure if the man behind it was down or still able to return fire.

"More loaded handguns are in my pack," Victor said, "but I only have the one mag for the rifle. We gotta get out of here."

Charity realized that Victor had been holding his breath against the gas. The two antique devices—the starlight goggles and the gas mask—didn't work together, and he'd opted for night vision over breathing.

"Let's go," she said, starting for the back of the house.

Victor fired another quick burst to cover her retreat, spraying the front of the house with high-velocity bullets. Then he too ran toward the back. Charity stopped at the door, turned, and fired several rounds to cover him. As Victor rushed through the door, Charity saw her rifle lying on a table in the kitchen. She grabbed it, fired two more shots from her Sig and followed Victor outside.

"Stay close behind me," Victor said, as he sprinted across the deck to the stairs at the corner. He stopped and fired two quick rounds at the back of the house, then the bolt locked open, the magazine empty. Rather than toss the rifle aside, Victor slung it over his head and shoulder, then pulled a handgun from the pack. He fired twice before starting down the steps.

Charity removed the gas mask and followed after him. The light of the moon provided enough light to see him, crouched on a landing and firing up through the boards of the deck. A moment later, he was sprinting across the yard, Charity following close behind.

Shouting voices and gunfire came from the house just as they reached the trees. Victor leaped over a log and came up with his big Kimber, methodically firing toward the house. The big .45 caliber rounds made a deafening boom.

Charity vaulted over the log and came up firing as well, though she couldn't see what she was shooting at.

"Stay close down the hill," Victor said, turning and moving off at a slower pace. "The first part is really steep."

Charity followed behind him, keeping a hand on his shoulder in the darkness. "Where're we going? Who was that shooting out front?"

"That was Chet," Victor replied, when they'd gotten to the bottom of the steepest part of the hill. "He's picking us up at a friend's house down below."

Victor stopped, and Charity could see him looking around. Shouts and the sound of footsteps running across the deck could be heard behind them. He struck out again, in a slightly different direction. After a moment, he stopped again and bent over.

A bright light came on at their feet and Charity recognized her laptop.

"I planted sensors along the tree line," he said, opening the breach on the grenade launcher. "Let me know if one goes off."

Charity knelt at the computer and checked the sensors. None were flashing. "Maybe they've given up."

Suddenly, the computer began beeping very softly and one of the sensor icons started to flash. "Or maybe not," she said. "That's number two. Will you be able to hit it from here through all these trees?"

Victor aimed the launcher almost straight up. "I can probably get close," he said, firing and reloading.

Way up the hill, an explosion split the night air, silencing the gunfire from above. Another sensor began blinking. "Number five, now."

Victor turned to his left, aimed, and fired again. A second explosion, this one far off to the left, lit up the night sky, as a third and fourth sensor began flashing.

"Numbers three and four," Charity said. "They're coming down the center."

"Get down behind that log," Victor said, reloading a third high explosive round. "Get ready to haul ass when this one goes off."

This time, Victor aimed directly through the trees, slightly uphill. When he fired, he instantly jumped over the log and pulled Charity down close to the ground.

A tremendous explosion rocked the whole hillside as the grenade exploded, igniting the dynamite. Dirt, rocks, and tree branches flew in all directions, followed by dozens of cracking sounds.

"Come on!" Victor shouted, closing the laptop and stuffing it in the pack. He tossed it over his other shoulder and grabbed Charity's hand, helping her to her feet. Together, they raced through the trees and underbrush, running downhill. A roaring sound—filled with loud cracks, as if an unseen giant were snapping tree limbs—spurred them on.

Looking back, Charity could see in the moonlight what could only be described as an apocalypse. Tall palm trees smashed to the ground, as if some unseen gargantuan were stepping on so many blades of grass. The trees became caught up, tumbling and snapping in two, as a massive slide of dirt, boulders, and parts of the house crashed them to the ground and pushed them down the hill.

Finally, they ran into a clearing, just as headlights from a car came up around the side of a house in the middle of the clearing.

"Get in!" Victor shouted, yanking open one of the car's back doors.

Charity climbed in, laying her rifle on the floor, and scooted across the broad bench seat. She levered her body through the open window, sitting on the doorframe and aiming her Sig over the roof.

Victor tossed the packs and rifle in, then jumped in with her. "Go! Go!" he shouted, as he too aimed his handgun up the hill.

Chet threw the car into reverse, grinding the gears. He backed to the left, up onto the grass, then shifted to first gear and spun the tires as the big Mercedes sedan took off down the steep driveway.

Charity and Victor pulled themselves back inside.

"What the hell did you do, Rene?" Chet asked, as he braked and put the old car into a skid at the bottom of the drive. "I heard a very large explosion up there."

"I think the blue house is gone," Victor said. "The explosion released all the fill dirt the house was built on."

"Aw, dat's a shame," Chet said as he accelerated up through the gears. "They had plans to rebuild and strengthen that house. Did you leave anything behind?"

"Just some trail sensors," Charity said, already sensing there was more to Chet than met the eye. "I bought them at a hunting outfitter."

"Nothing else?"

"Two expired CS grenades," Victor said. "They'll be hard to find in that debris."

"What about the Jamaicans?"

"Who the heck are you, anyway?" Charity asked, leaning forward in her seat.

Victor put a hand on her shoulder and she winced. "That's a question you're not allowed to ask," he said. His hand came away sticky with blood. "Were you hit?"

Charity sat back in the seat and put a hand to her own shoulder, wincing again. When she took her hand away, there was blood on it.

"I didn't feel it," Charity replied, sagging back in the seat, "but yeah, I do now."

Victor reached up and turned on the dome light, then began unbuttoning Charity's shirt, pulling it back to expose the wound. He gently pushed her forward to look at the back of her shoulder.

"Pretty big exit wound," he said, opening and rooting around inside his pack. "Doesn't look like it hit anything vital."

He ripped open a plastic bag and removed two large bandages and set them aside. Reaching into the pack again, he removed another, smaller plastic bag and tore it open.

"This is gonna burn, but I guess you already know that."

Charity leaned forward, giving him better access, and Victor covered the wound with the quick clotting sponge, pushing it in slightly. Charity jerked, but didn't cry out. He quickly wiped away the excess blood, peeled the backing off one of the bandages, and carefully placed it over the sponge, gently smoothing out the edges.

Charity leaned back in the seat again, and Victor did the same to the entry wound. "You probably should see a doctor," he said. "That exit wound will need stitches once that clotting sponge is pulled off. Otherwise, it'll leave a nasty scar."

Charity gritted her teeth through the searing pain, but grinned. "What? Guys don't dig scars?"

"I'm serious," Victor said, very concerned. "If you want, we can sail tonight. I know a doctor over on Jost Van Dyke."

"No doctors," Charity said.

"Well, we need to get you away from here," Victor said, then turned toward the front seat. "I'm guessing the Jamaicans are all dead, Chet. Is that a problem for you?"

"Not even a little bit," the old man answered. "They were evil."

"They're smuggling money," Charity said. "I overheard them talking. No idea why or where, though."

"Smuggling money?" Chet asked. "Or laundering it?"

Charity closed her eyes tightly against the burning pain in her shoulder. "Money laundering makes sense. My guess is they run drugs primarily."

"Laundered through whom?" Chet said, more to himself.

"You know everything that goes on here," Victor said, as Chet pulled into the driveway to their villa. "Has there been an uptick in drugs on the island?"

"No," the old man replied getting out and opening the back door for Charity. "Drugs are hard to find here, except the herb."

Chet helped Charity out of the car and Victor grabbed the bags and came around to join them. "I'll get the rest of our stuff," he said. "I want you to just sit down and rest. As soon as I make sure we have everything, we'll go down to *Salty Dog*. I'll feel safer there than here on land."

Chet carried the bags inside and on through the house, depositing them on the deck by the gate.

"Who is he?" Charity asked, as Victor helped her into one of the chairs in the living room.

Victor paused for a second, looking out the door. "Chet recruited me in ninety-seven, right out of college. He was OSS at the end of the war in Germany, and became a recruiter for the CIA in forty-eight."

"That'd make him at least—" Charity began.

"He's eighty-four," Victor interrupted. "Now, stay here while I grab our shit."

Victor disappeared into his room, as Chet came back inside. "No fire up there on the hill," Chet said. "But, I can hear sirens."

"Victor told me who you are," Charity said, standing and extending her hand to the old man.

He took her hand and said, "He must trust you a great deal to have told you that *and* his real name."

"He didn't tell me that part," she replied with a wink. "My real name is Charity Styles. I'm with DHS."

Chet stepped back. "I figured something like that."

"Thanks for all your help, Chet."

"It is we who should be thanking you," the old man said, looking out the broken French door. "I need to get Henri's car back to him. What will the two of you do now?"

"This isn't over," Charity said. "The Jamaicans delivered a million dollars to another boat, before taking me to that house. From what I heard, it was *another* million."

"Nobody on this island can clean that much drug money."

"My thought, exactly," Charity said, looking out on the bay with the old spook.

CHAPTER SEVENTEEN:

Safely aboard the *Salty Dog*, Victor took Charity to the larger forward head and did the best he could in dressing her wounds, including a scraped knee. Then they went up to the pilothouse, where they could see all approaches. Charity took her laptop out and powered it up, reducing the brightness in the darkened pilothouse. She connected to the modem on her own boat, giving her access to the mast-mounted camera.

"He's a legit developer," Victor argued. "Why would he get involved in shady stuff like drugs and money laundering?"

"Think about it," Charity answered, as she turned the camera toward the mega yacht. "What if we hadn't been here the other morning, when those men attacked Chet? Torching his shack was supposed to be an example to the homeowners. The Jamaicans would have pressed harder if they didn't agree to pay the protection money. At that point, a lowball offer to sell might have seemed like a better option."

"I get it," he said. "They strong-arm the locals, and he gets a discount price on the properties. In exchange, he launders money for the drug gang. But how can we prove it? The word of a couple of boat bums over that of a rich developer? Besides, that would expose us to what happened up on the hill."

"Before they blindfolded me," Charity began, switching to night optics on the masthead camera, "I saw something handwritten on the inside of the hull of the smaller boat that delivered me to the sport-fishing boat. Something about it only being illegal if you get caught."

Victor looked over her shoulder at the screen. The powerful optics zoomed in on the aft of the yacht. Charity moved the camera slowly toward the boats tied at the stern. The image continued to zoom in. The inside of the forward hull was barely visible.

"There!" Charity said. "That strip taped to the hull showing fish size limits."

"It's moving too much," Victor said. "I can't make anything out."

"Hold on," Charity said, pulling up a sub-menu and clicking on the Burst icon. The screen froze and she began clicking the Back button, looking for a clearer image. "Right there," she said, pointing at the screen.

"I'll be damned," Victor said.

"No, but that jerkwad and his captain will be."

"His captain?" Victor asked.

"He's in on whatever Whitaker's doing," she replied. "And it's not his first kidnapping. At least I don't think it is."

"Not following you."

Charity turned and looked up at him. "A couple of years back, before I started doing what I do now, McDermitt was kidnapped from his island, right out from under our noses. It was during the search for him that I disappeared. My handler gave me the full after-action report. The man who delivered Jesse to the kidnappers had a Texas accent. I heard Whitaker's captain speak. He's a Texan, and he fits the description to a tee."

"Still," Victor said, straightening. "That little saying written on that sticker might be on a dozen more."

"I scraped my knee on a rock as they were taking me down to that boat," Charity said, moving the camera again. "It was bleeding and I rubbed it on the combing around the rod storage box."

Victor knelt and looked closely at the screen. The boat was moving slightly, which completely distorted the image, but it was clear that there was a dark stain of some kind on the inside of the gunwale. Charity clicked the Burst icon again and sifted through the dozens of still images the camera captured in the one-second burst.

"Okay," Victor said, straightening and looking through the open hatch at the yacht. "What are we gonna do about it?"

"Do you have any more of that dynamite?"

"You want to blow up the ship?"

"Before the crew returns," she replied.

"That's just reckless revenge," Victor said. "What we should do is make sail and get the hell out of here. The Jamaicans are dead; there's no pressure on the islanders to give in to Whitaker's offer."

"And leave him to do the same thing to someone else?" Charity said, a bit more indignation than she wanted in her voice. "Look, I'm this close to chucking everything and sailing off with you, but I don't like loose ends."

Victor paced the deck, looking through the portholes that surrounded the pilothouse. Finally, he stopped and stood staring toward the yacht riding on two anchors behind them.

"You said they moved a million in cash aboard?"

"Not exactly," she replied, standing, and joining him by the navigation desk. "What I heard the guy say was to move *another* million aboard."

"So, two million?" Victor asked.

"Maybe more."

Victor looked down at her and grinned. "To Victor go the spoils."

She smiled. "Why not? It's not like the guy's going to suddenly do the right thing and donate the Jamaicans' drug money to Charity."

Victor grinned. "Not unfunny. We should go on the road with this act." Looking back out at the yacht, he thought it over. Finally, he turned toward Charity. "If we do this, there's no going back. Not for either one of us."

"I have to go back," Charity said. "Not permanently, but I have to make sure my friends know what I did and why. I have to know if I *have* to run, or want to."

"Your boat's known, and probably bugged nine ways to Sunday."

"I don't have to go back on my boat," she said. "But one bridge-burning at a time. How do we get the dirty money and blow the yacht?"

"I can get on the boat," Victor said, still looking back at the soulless yacht. "That's not the problem. I could hide a million bucks on *this* boat and it'd take a week to find." He pointed aft. "That's a damned big boat."

"The money's in crates on the launch deck," Charity said. "Probably several crates, and likely in small bills. It seemed as if the men who carried it were straining, so we're looking for wooden crates that weigh more than one man can lift easily."

"The launches are still tied to the stern," Victor said, thinking. "There's a chance it's still open—can't really see from here. Crates of provisions would normally be stored there, and anywhere else on board. It wouldn't look conspicuous. I'd just have to wrestle them into the water and drag them away."

"There's only two of them on the boat," Charity said. "It's a steel hull. I could hit the bow a couple of times, to divert their attention forward and cover you while you get away. But even rowing your dinghy, they might see you coming."

"I wasn't planning to go on top of the water," Victor said with a grin. "But look, this is way over-the-line crazy. The cops will be crawling all over this side of the island soon."

The sound of an outboard engine approaching interrupted them. They both turned toward the sound and saw a small pontoon boat in the moonlight. It was crossing the bay and approaching the yacht.

Charity brought the spotting scope up. "All of them aren't dead," she said, handing Victor the scope.

He looked toward the approaching vessel. "The boxer," he sneered. "Claude Whyte."

Charity lifted her rifle and went to the hatch, where she rested it in the crook of her left arm, on the cockpit deck. She switched on the optics and watched the approaching party boat. It was running with no lights, and slowing as it approached Whitaker's yacht.

Moving the scope to the mega-yacht, she saw Whitaker and the captain step down onto the huge swim platform. The pontoon boat stopped several feet away, and Whyte went forward, tossing a line to the yacht captain.

The man caught it but didn't haul the barge closer. He just held it as Whitaker and Whyte talked, several feet of water separating them.

"If I had any doubt," Victor said, "it's gone now."

All three men on the yacht turned, as Whyte pointed toward the villa. Whitaker waved the man closer, as the captain hauled the smaller boat in. Whyte stepped off, and the captain tossed the line back onto the pontoon boat, shoving it away from the yacht.

"He probably stole the boat," Charity said, watching the party barge drift away on the wind and falling tide. The three men disappeared inside.

"Okay, so now there's three of them on board," Victor said. "I can do you one better diversion. They have two anchors out; rather than plinking the bow with your rifle, think you can hit the anchor chains from here? It's flat calm out there."

"Sure, but a seven-six-two isn't gonna part those big chains."

"They will with a stick of dynamite strapped to each," he said, moving quickly to the aft cabin.

A few minutes later, he emerged, as Charity continued watching the yacht. The three men had appeared on the bridge, though she hadn't seen them go up the aft steps.

"I think the launch deck is still open," she said, looking over her shoulder as Victor placed a geared-up scuba tank on the deck.

"I'll put one stick on each anchor chain," he said, then lifted a small watertight box. "There's four sticks in here with a detonator and timer, set for four minutes. I'll activate it, then get the crates in the water." He clipped the watertight box to his BC. "His anchors are spread apart, and the chains are tense in the current. So, when you blow one chain, the yacht's gonna swing around on the second one. The second shot will likely be at a moving target."

Setting the rifle aside, she went to Victor and held him tight. "I'll take care of that. You just make sure you come back in one piece."

"I'll surface on this side," Victor said. "Just forward of their stern, where nobody will see me. Then I'll signal you that I'm ready, with an IR flash."

"Be careful," she said, then kissed him.

He returned the kiss, with more passion than during any of their previous lovemaking. Finally, he broke away, picked up his gear, and disappeared down the forward steps to the salon. Charity heard him open the hatch in his office, and moments later she could hear him crawling across the big foredeck, dragging his gear to the anchor chain.

Charity took up her position again, the rifle resting on her elbow as she watched the yacht. After a few minutes, she heard Victor climbing down his own anchor chain, then nothing. The three men were still on the bridge. Whitaker and Whyte appeared to be in a heated exchange.

The rich developer went to the side windows and stared up over *Wind Dancer*, toward the villa, his hands on his hips. He stood like that a couple of minutes, as if trying to decide something. Finally, he turned and started talking to Whyte again. He seemed to be asking pointed questions, almost interrogating the Jamaican. Whyte nodded or shook his head, occasionally elaborating or explaining his answer.

Looking back toward the villa, Whitaker said something, and Whyte immediately took his phone out and began tapping at the screen with his thumbs, obviously sending a text message.

A flash of light caught her eye through the scope. Charity moved the reticles to the stern and saw Victor's head bobbing ten feet forward from the side of the swim platform. The light flashed again. It came from the old starlight goggles he had mounted on his head, his scuba mask pulled down under his chin. Putting the crosshairs on the hull right beside him, she flashed the laser sight on and off. Victor jerked his head toward the red light hitting the hull, then lifted his fist, with his thumb extended and pointed forward.

It took Charity a moment to find the dynamite strapped to the anchor chain; it was further up than she thought he'd put it. The chain was moving ever so slightly, but in a consistent rhythm. Her finger tightened on the trigger, taking up the slack.

Charity slowed her breathing, noting the timing of the rise and fall of the chain and the tiny movement of the scope imparted on the rifle by each beat of her own heart. An Australian sniper on her old team had once told her that it was this unavoidable interaction that made sniping far more personal even than a garrote: the connection between one heart beating and another stopping.

The rifle recoiled against her shoulder, barely making a sound. But it brought the dull, throbbing pain from the bullet wound to a full roar.

The explosion overpowered the optics for a moment, but the light vanished as both ends of the chain dropped into the water. Charity quickly chambered another round and started looking for the other chain, knowing that the explosion could be heard, but not seen, from the yacht's bridge. Had one of the men been looking forward, they might have seen a flash of light, but the water extinguished everything almost instantly.

Surely they'd be looking forward now. Finding the second anchor chain, Charity followed it up and found the second charge. It was moving, but not up and down like the other one had been. The full weight of the tide pushing against the ship was now on the one chain. It was taut and slowly swinging away to her left. Just as the rifle recoiled again, she heard the yacht's engines start, but the second explosion drowned the sound of the engines momentarily.

Swinging the rifle to the bridge, she saw the captain at the wheel. She searched the rest of the bridge deck, but Whitaker and Whyte weren't there. A bright spotlight came on just outside the scope's vision, but she saw it through her open left eye. She looked over the scope and saw both men running forward, guns drawn, a bright spotlight illuminating the whole foredeck from above the bridge.

As the boat turned in the drifting current, Charity finally saw the stern. The large access door was open, a low light illuminating the inside. The compartment where the tenders were stored was directly below the aft sundeck, and looked like a busy place. Scanning the inside, she saw a lot of crates, two personal watercrafts, and the cradles for the two tenders, but no Victor.

Suddenly, the door began to close.

"Get out of there," she said through gritted teeth. "They're leaving. Forget the money."

The door closed completely.

Maybe he's already out, or never got in, she thought, going back to the scope, and scanning the water around the stern.

Not seeing Victor, she began a methodical sweep of the yacht, hoping to see him somewhere on the boat. Nothing.

On the foredeck, Whyte and Whitaker were running back to the outside ladder that went up to the bridge. At the helm, the captain was spinning the wheel to starboard.

She had to stop them. Aiming at the control panel in front of the captain, Charity fired.

At that moment, the transmissions engaged, turning two massive propellers. The yacht lurched forward, and Charity saw the captain's head jerk, saw the spray of blood on the console. He slumped over the side of his chair.

Charity watched in horror as the yacht began accelerating, the wheel still hard over to starboard, and no sign of Victor. The yacht picked up speed faster than Charity would have thought, the loud roar of its massive engines sounding like thunder rolling across a prairie.

She found Whitaker again, as he was climbing up the outside ladder to the bridge, unaware that his ship was turning toward the rocks at the end of Peterborg Peninsula. In frustration, she chambered a round and snapped a shot at him, just as the port side of the ship turned away from her, covering both him and Whyte from her rifle.

Charity moved the scope down along the back of the yacht and saw the launch deck door opening again. Her heart skipped a beat and relief flooded her when she saw Victor pushing one of the small Jet Ski type watercrafts down its slide.

Just as it entered the water, Victor jumped on and it nearly tipped over. There was a blinding flash from the launch deck. Charity dropped the rifle and stood up in the hatch as the sound of the third charge reached her ears, but a second larger blast dwarfed the first explosion.

Bright orange flames and black smoke rolled out of the stern, engulfing the water and continuing up to the heavens, orange flames and black smoke obscuring most of the stern. The whole ship seemed to shudder, as a second fuel tank exploded, blowing out the glass in the lower decks.

Victor's Jet Ski burst through the acrid black smoke and flames, speeding directly away from the crippled yacht. He turned the machine and nearly lost control, before getting it back on course toward *Salty Dog*.

Quickly, Charity climbed up to the cockpit and went over to the port side, where the boarding ladder was located. When Victor idled up, she noticed two large crates strapped onto the seat of the machine, his dive gear strapped on top of the rear one. When she realized Victor was sitting on one of the boxes she knew why he'd nearly dumped the Jet Ski. The thing was carrying the weight of three grown men.

She caught both handlebars of the Jet Ski and held the machine upright. Victor twisted his body, unbuckled the straps, and heaved his dive gear onto the deck. He strained to get one of the heavy chests up onto the deck. With less weight, the Jet Ski was more stable; Victor hefted the second box onto the deck easily, shoving the first further inboard.

He scrambled up the ladder, and Charity clung to him. "I thought you were gone," she sobbed, the emotion surprising her.

"Hoist with his own petard?" he asked, pushing her away. "Not a chance."

"Shakespeare?" Charity asked, seeing a different side to the man.

"You'll read anything, after fifty thousand miles at sea," Victor said, embracing her again. He pointed down to the little watercraft. "We gotta get rid of that, quick, then get these boxes below deck."

Another explosion rocked them and they turned toward the now burning yacht. It had straightened and was heading out to sea.

Victor wasted no time. He dove into the water, coming up next to the drifting Jet Ski. He started it and mashed the thumb throttle. The thing nearly leaped out of the water, as Charity watched him roar away after the yacht, wrapping the kill switch cord tightly around the throttle. Then, like a steer roper finishing his knot, he stood up, raising both hands, and fell backward off the Jet Ski.

Moments later, he came swimming back up to the ladder and climbed aboard. "Let's get these below and see what's inside," he said, lifting one of the crates and moving it to the hatch.

Charity looked out over the bay, toward open water. The burning ship was now fully engulfed in flames. Amazingly, the engines were still pushing it onward, increasing speed and fanning the flames higher. Behind it, the Jet Ski seemed to be giving chase. It would continue going straight until it ran out of gas or hit something.

Stacking the second box on the first, Victor went down the ladder with his dive gear. Charity shoved the top crate toward the hatch, so he could get his hands under it. Victor hoisted it onto his shoulder sideways and lowered himself inside. They quickly moved the second one down to the bridge deck, as well

Charity looked back once more at the yacht. It was now well past the tip of the peninsula, moving at well over twenty knots, she guessed.

As she watched, the whole thing erupted into a giant fireball.

Victor stuck his head up through the hatch. "Avgas for the turbine engines," he said. "That stuff's really flammable."

Together, they went back down into the pilothouse. From a drawer, Victor took out a small claw hammer and screwdriver. He quickly pulled the top off one of the crates and fell back on the deck, laughing.

"French-style green beans?" Charity said, lifting a can from the crate.

CHAPTER EIGHTEEN:

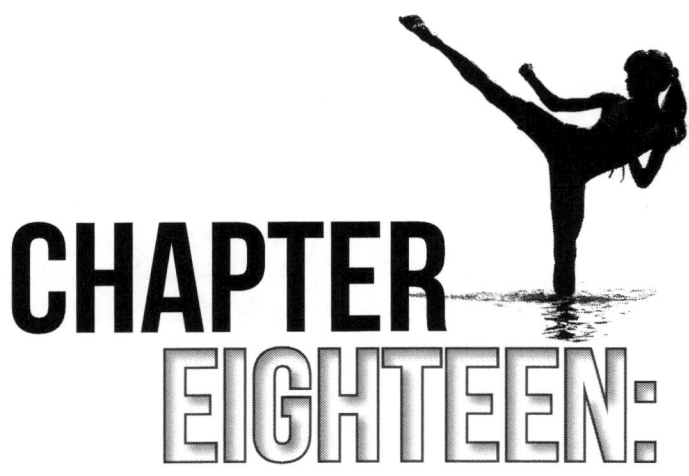

Throughout the morning, money floated ashore along Magens Bay, with the rising tide. Not long after sunrise, locals began turning out and scooping the floating bills out of the water, Chet among them. Many people handed wads of cash to Chet as they passed him. Islanders take care of their own.

Sergeant Lucien arrived at Magens Beach, and though he ordered people to stop, they mostly ignored him. Using a bullhorn, he ordered the people aboard the boats at anchor to come to the beach.

"We'd better go," Victor said. "Or they'll come out here."

They'd showered and redressed one another's wounds. Most of the swelling to Victor's face had gone down, and his hair hid the larger cut with the stitches, but it was still obvious that he'd been in a fight.

A short ride to the beach later, the two of them waded ashore, pulling the dinghy up onto the sand next to another one. Two couples stood next to it, talking to Lucien. When

Charity and Victor approached, they introduced themselves. They were from the big sport-fisher anchored close to the beach.

"What happened to yuh face?" Lucien asked Victor.

"He got drunk yesterday, and got into a fight at the Soggy Dollar, over on Jost Van Dyke," Charity said, inflecting a bit of feigned irritation in her voice.

Over the next hour, the sergeant took statements from each of them individually, asking pointed questions as to what they saw and heard. Charity and Victor told the same simple story they'd rehearsed, with just enough difference that it didn't sound rehearsed. They'd been out drinking, returned just a few hours before dawn, and were awakened by a huge explosion. All they'd seen when they got on deck was the big yacht heading out to sea, completely engulfed in flames.

"The yacht sank two miles offshore," Lucien explained. "And two bodies were found here in the bay, this morning. One was the owner of the yacht, who'd been shot in the chest. Nobody has reported hearing a gunshot, though."

"Oh, my," Charity said. "No, we didn't hear anything like gunfire."

"You know gunfire when you hear it, Mizz Fleming?"

"I am Cuban, Sergeant," she replied. "Yes, I am familiar with the sound of gunfire."

"Mmm," he replied. "The other body was the leader of a Jamaican drug gang that we've been watching. In the man's pocket, we found a silenced eight-millimeter handgun."

"Well," Victor said, "that would sure explain why nobody heard any gunshots."

"We haven't figured it all out yet," Lucien told the group, closing his notebook and putting it in a hip pocket, "but the gang had invaded one of the villas out near the tip of the peninsula and beat up a young couple. It seems the Jamaicans and the owner of the yacht were involved in some sort of illegal activity. All the money that came ashore seems to have come from the yacht. A large crate full of cash was found floating with debris from the boat."

"He didn't seem like the home invasion type when we met him," Victor said.

"Mmm," Lucien said, looking out over the bay. "Perhaps they had a disagreement. The house where the Jamaicans were staying was utterly destroyed late last night. Then, later, the yacht was blown up. We think the rich American killed most of the gang members, somehow, for whatever reason. There were several bodies on the scene up at Canaan."

"Was anyone else on the yacht?" Victor asked.

"We don't know," Sergeant Lucien replied. "Where it went down, it is a very deep trench. Too deep for divers."

One of the men from the sport-fisher spoke up. "We were planning to move on later today."

"That will be no problem," Lucien said, turning to the older man. "You are all free to go at any time. Thank you for your help."

Later, when they'd returned to *Salty Dog*, Victor opened a lazarette hatch on the aft deck and produced a pair of deck chairs. "So, what now?" he asked, offering Charity a seat.

They sat down with the chairs facing aft, looking out toward the open ocean they both wanted to be on.

After a moment, Charity looked over at Victor. "I have to go back."

He nodded his understanding. "And if I'm only half right?"

"I'm meeting with Jesse," she said. "He'll know what's going on."

"When?"

"Right away," she replied, turning away. "I'm leaving tomorrow."

"Then we should at least sweep your boat for transmitters today."

"Come with me, Victor."

"No," he replied. "It's out of the question."

They sat in silence for a long time. Finally, Victor sat forward, his elbows on his knees. "I have an idea," he said.

"Ahoy!" came a shout from up near the bow.

Victor sprang to his feet, reaching behind him for his Kimber.

Charity remained seated. "That's Henri," she said.

The old man came alongside, rowing a small wooden boat. "Permission to come aboard?"

Victor caught the line he tossed and tied it off to a deck cleat. Then he reached down and helped Henri up the ladder. "What are you doing out here?"

"I know you will be leaving soon," Henri said. "I didn't want you to leave before I could thank you."

"Thank us for what?" Charity asked.

"I am old," Henri said with a grin, kissing her lightly on both cheeks, "but I am no fool. Thank you both, from all of Peterborg."

"Have a seat," Victor offered. "I was about to open a bottle of wine, to toast our last evening in Magens Bay."

"Thank you, no," Henri said. "I can't stay. Lisette is preparing dinner, as we speak." He reached into a small bag he'd brought aboard and took out a tightly wrapped bundle. "This is for you both. Everyone on the beach this morning knows what you did. It is from all of us."

Victor slowly unwrapped the package. "We can't accept this, Henri," he said, showing Charity a box full of cash—mostly twenties and tens, but there were a few hundred-dollar-bills mixed in, as well.

"You must," Henri said, raising both hands. "My neighbors will be insulted if you refuse."

Charity smiled at the older gentleman. "Come down below for a moment, Henri?"

She led the way down into Victor's pilothouse. The crate full of canned green beans was left where they'd opened it. The other crate lay next to it, empty.

Charity went to the navigation desk and put a hand on a false panel in the bulkhead that Victor had shown her. She looked at him questioningly, and Victor nodded.

Opening the panel, she swung the false door aside, revealing four shelves, all stacked with the cash from the second crate. "This is half of what Victor liberated from Whitaker last night."

A slow smile spread across the old man's face. "Perhaps I will stay for one glass of wine and to hear a story."

Setting up another chair on the aft deck, Victor opened the bottle and together, he and Charity spun the tale about how the Jamaicans had attacked three times after burning Chet's Tiki bar. Henri was amazed that it was Charity who'd turned them back the first two times, and delighted that she'd tried to keep her promise of not hurting anyone.

"You can't tell anyone about this," Victor cautioned. "That money in your box? You should give that to William, to rebuild his house."

"It won't be needed," he said. "His insurance will cover rebuilding."

"Then donate it to a charity," Charity said. "An orphanage or something."

Henri smiled at her. "I will do just that, Gabriella. Lisette volunteers at an orphanage up in the hills."

After Henri left, Victor explained his plan to Charity and she listened closely, asking questions here and there.

"I don't know," she said, after he'd finished. "It might put you in danger."

"On the open water, danger can be seen for miles," he said. "And neither of our boats are speed demons. I plan to be in public places most of the time. I'll be fine. And after you do what it is you have to do, we can find each other again."

"Then we'd best get to work," she said. "A lot of things need to be moved back and forth."

They worked late into the night, first moving *Wind Dancer* alongside *Salty Dog* and tying the two boats together. By nightfall, they were exhausted. They shared Victor's large shower and then fell into his bed together, to make love one last time.

CHAPTER NINETEEN:

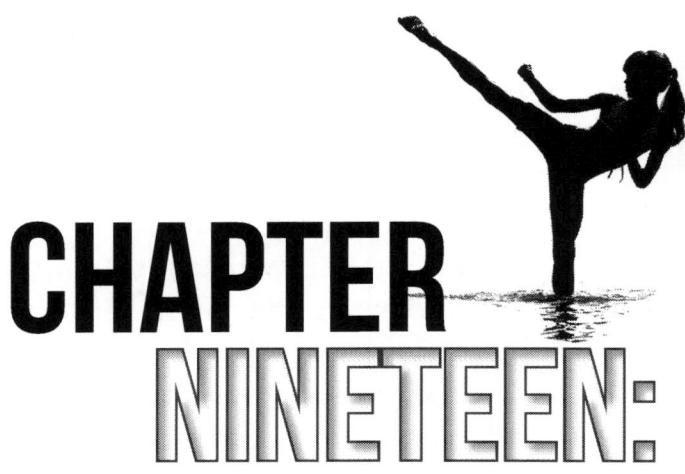

An hour before the sun was to rise, Charity and Victor stood at the rails embracing. "Two months," Victor said.

"Tortola," she said. "I'll be there."

"Try to find out about the disposition of your boat. I'm sure your half of the cash will be enough to buy it outright."

They each went to their helms and started the engines. A moment later, they kissed once more at the rails, then cast off. *Wind Dancer* moved away first, coming about slowly, and pointing her bow toward the bay opening, as if anxious to be underway. The anchor chain started rattling aboard the larger ketch. After several minutes, both boats began idling toward the bay mouth, *Dancer* going slower until the bigger boat caught up.

Thirty minutes later, as both boats neared the bay entrance, sunlight touched the tops of their masts. Both boats' sails unfurled, as their engines were shut down.

Wind Dancer's sails were set first, and she heeled over slightly, moving ahead of the bigger boat.

Holding the wheel steady, Charity studied the water ahead. The depth sounder showed the bottom dropping away precipitously, then it just disappeared from the screen, beyond the range of the device. Whitaker's megayacht was somewhere down there.

She turned on the VHF in case Victor called to her. He didn't.

Looking over, she saw him raise a thumb.

He shouted across the water: "Two months!"

Charity waved back, and then watched him turn away toward the rising sun. Tacking across the prevailing easterly wind, he barely slowed. She started to reach for the microphone, already feeling lonely, but stopped herself. Instead, she turned the wheel slightly to port, easing the sheets out to a broad reach, the wind at her starboard beam now. The boat turned sluggishly, something she'd have to get used to.

When she looked back, Victor was already far away. He had the sails close-hauled, beating to windward, and angling southeast toward the rising sun. When she looked forward again, a single tear slipped from the corner of her eye and rolled down her cheek.

She reached again for the radio, turning the volume up higher. He still didn't hail her. Turning on the autopilot, she went forward to put up more canvas. With the sun at her back and the wind abeam, she ran up all the sails the boat had.

Salty Dog carried more individual sails, but the combined sail area wasn't a whole lot more than the *Dancer's*. Each sail being smaller in size, they were a lot easier for one person to handle manually. Back at the helm, Charity adjusted each sail for optimum performance and soon she had Victor's boat careening along at ten knots, taking the waves almost broadside.

On *Wind Dancer*, waves like these pushed and nudged her this way and that. But, *Salty Dog* simply plowed through them using brute strength and sheer size to toss the water away from the wide bow, sometimes in great cascades, a perpetual rainbow off the starboard bow.

Aside from traveling back to the States incognito, *Salty Dog's* faster hull speed was another reason they'd switched boats. It was only a knot or two difference, but that meant a lot less time on a long run like Charity was now starting.

She liked the feel of the big, heavy ketch and turned off the autopilot to take the wheel again. A fine mist of salt spray came back from the bow, nearly fifty feet ahead of where she stood in the aft cockpit. She licked her lips, relishing the taste of new ocean.

One by one, the stars began to disappear as the sun peeked above the horizon behind her. When she looked back again, *Wind Dancer* was merely a dot on the horizon, heading east to the British Virgin Islands. Ahead, she had nearly a thousand nautical miles to reach her destination. She'd plotted stops in a few deserted coves along the way to rest, and figured she'd arrive in the Florida Keys within a week.

Going home, she thought—or, at least, the only place that had felt like home for a very long time.

She went forward to where her pack lay behind the dodger, out of the spray. Opening it, she removed her laptop and powered it on. When it booted up, she opened and reread the message she'd saved from Jesse, his reply to the phony charter request:

> *There's an island I swim to every Monday, Wednesday, and Friday morning. I see a lot of individual butterflies on the east shore.*

The man had understood her cryptic message.

If you'd like to receive my twice a month newsletter for specials, book recommendations, and updates on coming books, please sign up on my website:

WWW.WAYNESTINNETT.COM

THE CHARITY STYLES
CARIBBEAN THRILLER SERIES

Merciless Charity
Ruthless Charity
Reckless Charity

THE JESSE MCDERMITT
CARIBBEAN ADVENTURE SERIES

Fallen Out
Fallen Palm
Fallen Hunter
Fallen Pride
Fallen Mangrove
Fallen King
Fallen Honor
Fallen Tide
Fallen Hero
Rising Storm (Summer, 2017)

The Gaspar's Revenge Ship's Store is now open. There you can purchase all kinds of swag related to my books.
WWW.GASPARS-REVENGE.COM

Made in the USA
Columbia, SC
01 December 2018